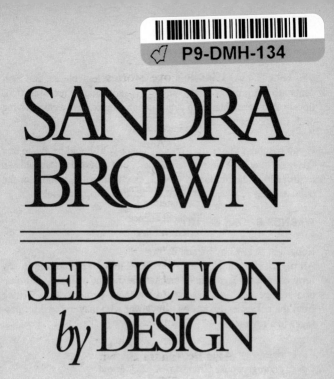

SANDRA BROWN

SEDUCTION
by DESIGN

WARNER BOOKS

An AOL Time Warner Company

WARNER BOOKS EDITION

Copyright © 1983 by Sandra Brown
All rights reserved. No part of this book may be reproduced in any form or by any electronic or mechanical means, including information storage and retrieval systems, without permission in writing from the publisher, except by a reviewer who may quote brief passages in a review.

Cover design by Jackie Merri Meyer
Cover photograph by Graphistock - R.J. Muna

Warner Books, Inc.
1271 Avenue of the Americas
New York, NY 10020

Visit our Web site at www.twbookmark.com.

An AOL Time Warner Company

Printed in the United States of America

Originally published in hardcover by Warner Books.

First Paperback Printing: March 2002

10 9 8 7 6 5 4 3 2 1

Dear Reader,

For years before I began writing general fiction, I wrote genre romances. *Seduction by Design* was originally published almost twenty years ago.

This story reflects the trends and attitudes that were popular at that time, but its themes are eternal and universal. As in all romance fiction, the plot revolves around star-crossed lovers. There are moments of passion, anguish, and tenderness—all integral facets of falling in love.

I very much enjoyed writing romances. They're optimistic in orientation and have a charm unique to any other form of fiction. If this is your first taste of it, please enjoy.

Sandra Brown

SEDUCTION
by DESIGN

CHAPTER | 1

Miss Ashton," Hailey said, pressing down the lighted button on the intercom panel.

"Miss Ashton, this is Dawson." Hailey Ashton could tell by the scratchy static and the background noise that the security guard was speaking into his pocket pager. "You'd better get over here to the Sidewinder quick. All hell's broken loose and no one can seem to determine exactly what's happened."

This was an emergency call, Hailey realized at once. The steady, reliable Mr. Dawson was obviously shaken. "What's going on?" she asked with professional crispness.

"Well, this guy here is raising Cain, yelling at everyone like a banshee. Says something's happened to his daughter. From what I can tell, the kid dashed into the ladies' rest room and holed up. This character has attracted quite a crowd. People are beginning to speculate all sorts—"

"I'll be right there."

"Do you want me to send a cart for you? It's hotter than—"

"No, I'll run through the compound," Hailey said quickly. "Dawson, try to calm everyone down. Especially the father."

"Right."

He clicked off his transmitter and Hailey dashed out the door after calling, "Take over, Charlene," to her assistant. The glass cubicle of Hailey's office was near the front gate of the amusement park. The September heat slammed into her chest as she adroitly weaved her way through the throng of guests who, with their cameras and children in tow, were streaming through the turnstiles into the park.

One customer was holding up the line by arguing with the gate attendant over a discount ticket. The frantic employee looked up with relief as Hailey sped by. "Miss Ashton—"

"Are you having trouble, sir?" Hailey went straight to the heart of the matter to save time. Her mind was on the emergency at the Sidewinder.

"Yeah," the man answered belligerently. "She says I can't get my little one in on this discount ticket. He's only three. He won't be able to go on the big rides anyway. I thought—"

"Please, sir, take your family on in. I'm sure that ticket is acceptable," Hailey said hurriedly. Her decision wasn't fair to the park's management, or to the employee who hadn't been backed up, or to the other guests who had paid full ticket price for their three-year-olds, but Hailey had an emergency to attend to. She'd make it up to the disgruntled employee later.

Barely nodding in response to the man's effusive thanks, she let herself into a gate through the tall, gray wooden fence that separated the public areas from the employees' compound in the center of the park. Serendipity Amusement Park was crowded on this Saturday afternoon, and the greater the number of people, the greater the probability that crises would crop up. As Director of Guest Relations, Hailey was accustomed to handling minor emergencies instigated by either God or man.

Her low-heeled sandals weren't conducive to jogging, but she moved at a brisk trot across the expanse of asphalt that fairly shimmered in the unseasonable heat. Her white skirt swirled around her slender legs. She could feel perspiration dampening her green cotton shirt, where the park's emblem was discreetly appliquéd on her breast pocket just under her plastic name tag. Thank goodness she had worn her hair up in a topknot today. Otherwise the copper-colored, shoulder-length skein would be curling riotously in the humid heat.

Hailey reached the opposite side of the compound in record time and went through the gate. The Country Roads Theater where college performers provided a musical revue six times a day had just been emptied and she was absorbed by the milling crowd.

A gracious smile hid the turmoil in her mind. *A little girl hiding in a rest room? What could have hap-*

pened to her? Despite her haste, Hailey bent down to pick up a cigarette butt someone had negligently dropped. An employee who was seen stepping over any form of litter on the park grounds was fired immediately. A veritable army of maintenance workers in bright green uniforms kept the park as clean as a grandmother's parlor.

Hailey passed one of the many large gift shops that sold posters, T-shirts, and souvenir coffee mugs, as well as other commemorative items of the Great Smoky Mountains, the state of Tennessee, and Gatlinburg itself. It was doing a thriving business.

The crowd in the gift shop couldn't compare, however, to the curious crowd gathered around the ladies' rest room near the Sidewinder. The roller coaster was of such fearsome proportions that Hailey had never dared ride it. She paid scant attention to it now as she plunged into the throng.

"Excuse me, excuse me, please," she said courteously but firmly as she elbowed her way through the crowd. "Excuse me." She edged around a man eating a dripping ice cream bar and virtually stumbled into Dawson.

"Dawson," she said, tapping him on the shoulder to get his attention over the racket.

He spun around. "Miss Ashton, thank—"

"Is this who we've been waiting an eternity for?"

The voice was hard and scornful, impatient, and obviously furious. It also implied that Hailey hadn't been worth the wait. She turned around to meet steely gray eyes under scowling dark brows.

"I'm Hailey Ashton, Director of—"

"Guest Relations," he mocked as his searing eyes swept down and across her breast to locate her identification badge. "Spare me the title. I want some action." Only then did he raise his eyes back to hers. The anger in his gaze seemed to flicker for a heartbeat as he stared at her. He paused, blinking, then said, "Something has happened to my daughter and I'm surrounded by a bunch of bungling incompetents." His lips hardly moved as he spoke.

"Please calm down, sir, and tell me what happened," Hailey said authoritatively. "Your loss of control isn't helping either yourself or your daughter, is it?"

Had the situation not been so urgent, Hailey would have tempered her rebuke. This man certainly didn't look the type who would take criticism lightly, if at all. But his insults and anger were only adding to the problem.

He glared down into Hailey's cool green eyes. Her control battled his rising impatience and won. He conceded grudgingly and continued in a more rational tone.

"We were standing in line for that thing. . . ." He gestured toward the roller coaster. "Suddenly, for no apparent reason, my daughter went as pale as a ghost and started screaming. Then she ran into the rest room.

I ran after her, but was met at the door by a militant attendant who wouldn't let me in. I—"

"She's still in there?" Hailey asked Dawson, turning her back on the man. Dawson nodded. "What's her name?" she asked of the father, whose frustration had trebled while Hailey ignored him.

"Her name!" he roared. "For God's sake, what difference does that make? Something dreadful may have happened to her and you stand here like some robot and ask me—"

"Her name."

He raked his fingers through his dark hair, which had already been mussed from similar handling. "Her name is Faith, dammit. Faith."

"Thank you," Hailey said. She hastened toward the door of the rest room and called over her shoulder. "Dawson, please disperse this crowd. Send for a cart and notify the infirmary that I may be bringing someone in." She didn't look back to see if her orders were being carried out. She knew they would be. Nor did she glance back at the tall, broad-shouldered man who she knew was stalking her like a combat soldier bent on revenge.

She went into the cool rest room and took a moment to adjust her eyes to the dim interior after the blinding sunlight outside. The attendant looked at her with unqualified welcome. Before Hailey could ask her anything, she rushed to tell what she knew.

"Miss Ashton, there was a crowd of ladies in here. I was cleaning one of the sinks when this little girl comes running in screaming and crying. She locked herself up in that last stall. I've been trying to get her to open the door, but she won't come out. I even stood on the commode in the stall next to her and looked over. She's just crouched in the corner sobbing her little heart out. That wild man came running in here, carrying on something terrible. The other ladies started screaming, thinking he was a pervert or something chasing that frightened little thing. I sent everyone out. I'm telling you, I—"

"Thank you, Hazel," Hailey said, breaking off the explanation which she feared might go on forever. "Why don't you wait for me outside? If I need you, I'll call. And please don't let anyone else in here."

"Yes, ma'am."

Hailey walked to the last stall and pushed gently on its latched door. "Faith? Are you all right?" There was no response except for the weeping she had heard since coming into the rest room. "Faith? Please let me in. I want to help you. Your father is very worried about you."

There was a slight cessation of the crying. A few sniffles. Some dry sobs. Then a gentle hiccuping. Hailey took advantage of the quiet. Speaking softly she said, "My name is Hailey. Whatever is wrong, you can tell me." Intuitively, she added, "No one else has to know the problem if you prefer. Not even your father." Hailey hoped that was a promise she would be able to keep, but at the moment it was crucial that she get the child to open the door.

"You . . . you won't tell anybody?" The question was faint, barely audible.

"Not if you don't want me to."

"It's embarrassing." Another sob. "But it hurts."

Hailey was growing more anxious by the moment. She glanced over her shoulder, afraid that the man would come barging in the rest room despite her orders that no one interrupt. "What hurts?"

She heard the rustle of clothing before the metal lock was released. The door opened inward and a girl about eleven years old stood in the opening. She was neatly dressed in tennis shoes and shorts and was holding a matching blouse over her thin chest with tight fists.

Dark brown ponytails tied with pink ribbons sprouted from both sides of her head. Through a pair of tortoise-shell eyeglasses, she looked up at Hailey with tearful gray eyes. Her father's eyes, Hailey noted and wondered why she remembered the color of his eyes.

"Hello, Faith," Hailey said and stood aside in a silent invitation for the girl to come out of the stall.

"Hi." She came out and stood self-consciously in front of Hailey, staring at the floor.

"Can you tell me what the matter is? What's hurting you?"

The child licked her lips and Hailey saw the flash of metal braces in her mouth. "I got . . . uh . . . a bee stung me."

"Oh no," Hailey said, instantly concerned. "Are you allergic to them?"

Faith shrugged. "I don't think so. I mean, I don't think I'm gonna die or anything." There was a slight catch in her tremulous voice. "It just stings," she finished softly.

"Where did it sting you?"

"Out by the Sidewinder."

Hailey bit her lip to keep from smiling, "I know. I mean, where on your body?"

"Oh." Faith looked up quickly at Hailey, then away just as quickly. "Here," she said and lowered her shirt with a yank, as though she might change her mind if she thought about it longer.

Hailey saw two red welts on the tender young breast that showed the first signs of budding womanhood. Suddenly she understood. There had been no mother with the anxious father. When the bee stung her, Faith had been too modest to tell him about where she'd been hurt.

Hailey's heart went out to the child. She remembered from her own adolescence how intensely she had craved privacy, how painfully aware and embarrassed she had been of each change in her body.

She walked to a sink and soaked a paper towel with cold water. She tried to interject a matter-of-factness into her tone. "How do you suppose the bee got there?" she asked with a smile.

"I was reaching up to touch one of the flags on the railing. There are some bushes there."

"Honeysuckle."

"Yeah, that stuff smells real good. Anyhow, he must have flown in through the armhole of my blouse." Her lips began to quiver again. "Do you think my daddy will be mad at me? I think I acted sorta dumb."

Hailey suppressed another smile while she pressed a wet towel to the narrow chest. She held it for a moment against the fiery welts until Faith took the towel in her own hand. "I think he'll be relieved to know it was nothing more than a bee sting," Hailey reassured her.

"Not that the sting isn't painful. Don't let him worry you, though. Men don't understand how we women feel about such things, do they?"

Wide-eyed, Faith shook her head at the beautiful lady who seemed to understand everything. "No. He doesn't understand anything. He thinks I'm still a baby."

"Well anyone can see that you're practically grown up. What did he expect you to do? Tear off your blouse in front of everyone and start yelling that a bee had stung your breast?"

Her silliness produced the hoped-for results. Faith giggled. Hailey pressed her advantage. "Why don't we slip your blouse back on? Keep holding that cold towel there. We'll ride in a golf cart to the infirmary and I'll put this fantastic ointment on the stings that's guaranteed to make them stop hurting. Then we'll have a Coke. How does that sound?"

Faith looked nervously toward the door and Hailey

added, "The crowd will be gone. I had one of the security guards send everyone away. But we really shouldn't hog the rest room, you know."

Faith laughed. She put on her blouse and Hailey helped her with the buttons. Faith folded her arm across her chest so she could keep the cold compress in place. Then Hailey gave her a cool cloth to bathe her face. The only visible signs of her distress were her puffy eyes and reddened nose.

Hailey draped an arm across Faith's slight shoulders and they went through the door. As Hailey had hoped, the curious onlookers had scattered. Faith's father stood frozen, staring at the door, but he came to life the moment they stepped outside. He stalked toward them.

"Faith, are you all right?" he demanded.

"Yes, Daddy. I'm fine," she said timidly.

"What in the— world . . . made you behave like that?"

Hailey interrupted the cross-examination, feeling it would be better postponed. "I'm taking Faith to the infirmary in the golf cart. I think she's fine, but I want to make sure." She ushered the girl over to the golf cart Dawson had requested for them.

"Now look here, Miss—"

"Mr. Dawson will be glad to show you the way," Hailey told the man coldly as she engaged the gears of the small cart and steered it around a group of boisterous teenagers. Had she looked back, she would have seen him standing with his hands on his hips, glowering at her as though it would give him the greatest pleasure to strangle her.

By the time Hailey and Faith arrived at the infirmary in the compound, they had become fast friends. They were chatting amiably when they stepped into the small brick building. Since the nurse was occupied with a middle-aged man who was suffering from overexertion, Hailey took Faith into one of the small treatment rooms.

"Tell me if I hurt you," she murmured as she softly applied the sticky ointment from a silver tube to the welts on Faith's breast. No sooner had she finished than they heard the front door being thrust open and footsteps rushing into the reception room. "That's Daddy," Faith said miserably. "He's gonna be so mad at me."

"You let me handle him. Would you like that Coke now?" Hailey asked calmly.

"Yes, please. Do you mind if I drink it in here?"

Hailey smiled, understanding Faith's reluctance to face her father just yet. "You may stay in here as long as you like."

She shut the door behind her and faced the man who was pacing back and forth in front of the nurse's desk. "Where is she?" he asked peremptorily. Hailey knew she had never encountered a man as rude as this one.

"She's in the treatment room," she replied and went to a refrigerator on the opposite wall. "I told her I'd bring her a Coke."

"A Coke!" he exploded. "She's drinking a Coke at a time like this?"

Hailey calmly ignored him as she flipped off the tab on the can and carried it without another word into the other room. Faith was sitting on the examination table reading the antismoking posters on the wall and swinging her long, thin legs.

"Thank you," she said politely when Hailey handed her the drink.

Hailey eyed the girl carefully as she asked, "Faith, where is your mother?"

Faith lowered her head and mumbled into her chest, "She died. A few months ago." Hailey had thought as much. "I think I should tell your father about the stings, don't you?" Faith nodded and Hailey patted the girl on her bare knee before slipping through the door again and shutting it firmly behind her.

Faith's father was sitting on the edge of the imitation leather sofa, but he bolted off it when Hailey closed the door. "You may want to sit back down," she said. "I have a form to fill out."

She went behind the desk, trying not to notice that he was fuming. She took the necessary accident report form out of the desk drawer and put it into the typewriter.

"Now, what—"

"To hell with your bloody forms, Miss Ashton. I want to know about my daughter—now." The voice wasn't as loud or exasperated as it had been earlier.

But it was twice as deadly. He had moved away from the couch to stand directly beside her.

She looked up at him. He was leaning on his palms, his arms spread wide as he bent over the desk. His face was close to hers. Alarmingly close. For the first time, she saw him as a man, and not a contrary guest who had turned an otherwise routine day into a calamitous one.

His arresting eyes were as cold and determined as she had noticed before. His nose was long and slender and flared slightly at the nostrils. His mouth was wide; it was thinned now in a resolute expression, but when relaxed it would be full and sensuous. His chin and jaw were hard and stubborn and indicated a force of will dangerous to anyone brave enough to parry with it. His hair was still mussed, but lay against his head in well-cut strands that were attractively streaked with silver at the temples.

A blue polo shirt stretched across his wide chest and the muscles of his tanned upper arms. His casual slacks, a darker blue than his shirt, fit easily over his taut, narrow hips and hard thighs. At the base of his leanly corded neck, through the open collar of his shirt, Hailey could see a hint of the dark hair that surely matted the awesomely masculine chest.

Leaning over her as he was, he was much more intimidating than he had been when she was surrounded by a crowd of people. His strength and purpose were nothing to tangle with. Only a fool would try. His very maleness was a palpable force. She swallowed and, relying on her professional demeanor, said, "Faith was stung by a bee. I have applied an antiseptic-analgesic ointment to the bites. She's resting."

His breath escaped with a sigh of relief. He straightened, wiping his damp forehead with the back of his hand. When he had realized that his daughter was in no real danger, Hailey again fell victim to his impaling, incisive eyes. "What the hell was all the fuss about then? Why didn't she just tell me what had happened to her instead of running away and hiding like that?"

"The bee flew under her blouse. It stung her on her breast." She looked at him steadily. He stared back at her. No emotion was apparent in his gray eyes or on his firm mouth. "Your daughter is becoming a young lady, Mr.—"

"Scott."

"Mr. Scott. She's naturally self-conscious about the changes her body is undergoing. Being frightened by pain, she was mortified by the location of the stings and too embarrassed to tell you."

"But that's crazy. I know what a female breast looks like."

For some reason Hailey didn't want to put a name to, she suddenly became hot and breathless. She ridiculed herself for acting as juvenile as Faith.

"It may be crazy to you, Mr. Scott, but to an impressionable, sensitive girl Faith's age, it would have been devastating to . . . to show herself to you."

"I'm her father," he said, his impatience with female logic apparent.

"Even so, Mr. Scott. I know it's hard for you to understand, but please try. Faith is very upset. She's afraid you'll be angry with her."

He cursed under his breath and flung himself down on the sofa again. He stroked his stubborn chin several times with a frustrated hand. He was a man striving to understand something he had no experience of. When he looked up at Hailey again, she saw something softening in his steely gray eyes. "I guess I overreacted as violently as Faith."

Hailey treated him to a real smile. "That's understandable. Forgive me, but I asked Faith about her mother. She told me that you have recently lost your wife."

"She wasn't my wife." Seeing Hailey's sudden loss of color and the stunned expression on her face, he clarified his remark. "She was my wife when Faith was born, but we were divorced soon after. Faith lived with her mother all that time. Monica was killed in a boating accident several months ago and Faith came to live with me." His hard mouth slanted in a self-deprecating smile. "I'm still learning about parenting, you see."

Hailey glanced down at her hands, then shyly back up at him. "Single-parenting is an unenviable job for anyone. Under the circumstances I can see why you and Faith both would have adjustments to make."

Why was she talking to this man so candidly about such a personal subject? Still, he had initiated it, hadn't he? Dare she give him one more word of unasked-for advice? "Please remember one thing, there is nothing more patience-taxing, sensitive, or emotionally delicate than an adolescent girl."

His thick brows lowered over eyes sparkling now with mischief. "Except an adolescent boy trying to make a move on an adolescent girl."

Dark lashes momentarily screened Hailey's green eyes. A blush colored her cheeks, so recently pale, with flattering color. Rather than meet his probing eyes, she turned back to the typewriter and, in a no-nonsense voice, said, "I must get back to my office, but first I have to complete this form." She set the proper margin on the typewriter, then inquired tersely, "Your full name?"

"Scott. Tyler Scott."

Her hands froze on the keys. Her mouth went as dry as cotton. Her heart leaped into her throat. Her whole body shook with a slight tremor.

In her peripheral vision she saw Tyler Scott get up off the sofa and walk around the desk to stand directly in front of her. Her upraised eyes took in the designer belt at his waist, his long, tapering torso, and impressive chest, the tanned column of his throat.

When her eyes locked with his as he stared down at her, she quailed under his triumphant expression. "That's right, Miss Ashton," he said softly. "I own this place."

CHAPTER 2

The accident report form was ripped out of the typewriter without the benefit of the paper release. With an accuracy that would have made Wilt Chamberlain applaud, the viciously balled-up paper was sent sailing through the air into the dead center of a metal trash can.

"I think we can dispense with the mandatory report this time, don't you, Miss Ashton?" he asked coolly. "After all, the accident forms eventually wind up on my desk and I already know the details of this incident. I hardly think Serendipity can be held responsible for the actions of one lone bee, who was only doing what comes naturally to bees. I will, however, see that the flowering shrubs are sprayed one more time before the park closes for the season to prevent something like this from happening again."

As he talked, he paced around the office, hands in his pockets, studying with infinite interest the posters and notices tacked to the wall. Hailey sat petrified at the typewriter. What had she said to this man? Had she been rude? Yes, she had been. She had deliberately withheld information about his daughter. She had made him walk all the way from the Sidewinder to the center of the compound. God, she'd be lucky to have her job this time tomorrow. He might fire her right now.

"What I *do* have to consider carefully, however, is how my employees responded to an emergency situation. I'd be derelict in my responsibility to Serendipity's guests if I didn't, wouldn't I?"

For the first time since he had identified himself, Hailey spoke, and her voice was little more than a croak. "Yes, you would," she agreed dismally. Here it comes, she thought. He'll either chew me out and put me on probation or he'll dismiss me outright. *But he'd been damned provoking!* she defended herself righteously.

Bracing herself for his lecture, she was surprised when he went toward the door of the treatment room and tapped lightly. "Faith? Are you all right now? I'm still waiting for that ride on the Sidewinder."

The door opened and a chagrined Faith walked out. Tyler Scott smiled at her gently and chucked her under the chin. "Hi. You had me worried. Are you feeling better now?"

"Yes, Daddy. I'm sorry I acted so dumb. I was too . . . I mean . . . It was . . ."

"No need to explain. Miss Ashton has done that for you. Thank her now, and let's go. Unless you want to spend the rest of the day in the infirmary," he teased.

"No." Faith giggled. She looked like she might reach around her father's waist and hug him, but she didn't. Instead, she turned to Hailey, who was still seated in the chrome and plastic chair with the squeaky casters as if she had been fixed there permanently.

"Thank you, Hailey. Gee, I don't know what I would have done if you hadn't come along. You're super."

"Thank *you* for the compliment. I'm glad I was available. Do you think your stings will hurt you anymore before you get home?"

"No, they don't hurt at all."

"Watch them for swelling or additional redness. Some insect bites can be serious." Hard as it was, she faced the flinty eyes that she could feel boring into her. "You may want to pick up some kind of analgesic ointment for her, Mr. Scott."

"Very good advice, Miss Ashton. What kind?"

Hastily she scribbled the name of a salve on a piece of paper and extended it to him. Instead of taking the paper, his strong fingers wrapped around her wrist. "I'll be in touch," he said in a low, threatening voice. For emphasis, his thumb stroked upward and pressed the center of her palm. It wasn't until he had taken the slip of paper with his other hand, that her wrist was freed.

"Faith?" He opened the door and ushered his daughter out into the heat while Hailey shivered with a cold foreboding.

How could she have made such an atrocious blunder? From the first time she saw Tyler Scott, he had irritated her. She *had* been rude to him. She *had* taken a perverse pleasure in increasing his anxiety. She *had* felt a smug satisfaction at making him walk when there was plenty of room for him to ride in the golf cart. Spitefulness didn't usually characterize Hailey Ashton.

She wrote the nurse a note explaining briefly what had happened and left the infirmary. Should she call the other department heads and warn them that their employer was in the park? No. She had already gotten Mr. Scott's ire up. Until she heard from him, she'd keep a low profile and only hope that her colleagues fared better should they encounter the owner of the park.

She walked through the compound quickly, not having to concentrate on where she was going. For the past four years Serendipity had been her turf. She knew its walkways, its waterways, its shops, eateries, theaters, and other attractions like the back of her hand. To do her job well, she had acquainted herself with every aspect of the park's operation.

Doing things well was Hailey's most ardent ambition. She was known for her competence. Wouldn't everyone be surprised when they learned that she had lost her job for bullying a guest who just happened to be Tyler Scott?

She had been at Serendipity for a year when it was sold to Scott Enterprises of Atlanta and it became only a small part of that huge conglomerate. The Scott empire included real estate companies, sawmills, a computer firm, a shopping center, a housing development, as well as various other properties.

It was a standing joke around Serendipity that Tyler Scott wasn't a real person, but rather a generic name given to a group of doddering old men. Since no one had ever seen him, and all his business transactions were conducted by a battery of subordinates, it was speculated that Tyler Scott, the man, didn't exist.

Hailey's private smile was rueful. Tyler Scott was most definitely a man. In no way could the adjective "doddering" be used to describe him, not with those shoulders and that chest. No, he had been all too real.

What would such a man do with an employee who was supposedly an expert in handling the guests of his multiacre amusement park, whose sole purpose was to see to the guests' well-being and enjoyment, but instead had behaved in a curt, uncompromising, unsympathetic way? What indeed?

It was after nine o'clock when she finally arrived home. Her last official duty of the day had been to see that all one hundred and thirty Boy Scouts on a special field trip were given Serendipity bumper stickers, which they promptly began sticking to each other.

Her sandals were left at the front door, her blazer was dropped on a chair. Automatically going into the kitchen, she checked the refrigerator to see what forgotten treasure she might uncover, but was vastly disappointed. Another omelet tonight, she groaned mentally as she made her way down the darkened hallway toward her bedroom.

She had just stripped out of her uniform when the telephone rang. "Hello."

"Will you accept the charges on a call from Ellen Ashton?"

"Yes," Hailey replied wearily.

"Hi, sis."

Hailey was annoyed that Ellen had called collect again, but pushed aside her uncharitable thoughts with a guilty sigh. Just because she had had a terrible day, that didn't mean she should take her frustrations out on her sister.

"Hi, Ellen. What's going on?" She knew before asking that she was letting herself in for a lengthy discourse on the latest events in Ellen's life. And at her expense. She sat on the bed and prepared to listen.

Hailey barely credited herself with being moderately attractive, but had always felt that her sister, younger by two years, was stunning. Hailey's hair was a glowing copper, but Ellen's flamed. Hailey was tall and fashionably slender, but she thought of herself as skinny, the way she had been as a figure-conscious teenager. Ellen hadn't been cursed with adolescent coltishness. She had gone from plump girlhood to voluptuous womanhood without any awkwardness in between.

Hailey was dependable. Ellen was hopelessly irresponsible. But she was beautiful and bubbly, and everyone adored her. If her flightiness often cost her a good job, she soon charmed someone else into hiring her, despite mediocre skills.

"It sounds like you're happier at this job than at the last," Hailey interjected when Ellen paused for breath after several talkative minutes.

"Oh yes! The people are much nicer. The women who worked in that other office were so mean to me. I think they were jealous. They told the boss bad things about me. I had to leave for my own peace of mind."

Hailey was suspicious about how Ellen's actual leaving had come about, but she didn't contradict her sister's version. Ellen should never be required to work. It didn't suit her personality. She should find an indulgent rich man to pamper and spoil her for life.

"I've made some new friends, Hailey, and we've been going out every night and having a ball."

"That's wonderful, Ellen."

"There's a big party I've been invited to next week at the country club. It's going to be fabulous! All the best people will be there." Hailey flinched at Ellen's snobbery. "Anyway, Hailey, I have one teeny-weeny problem."

Hailey knew immediately what that teeny-weeny problem was. "I need a new dress, Hailey. And I haven't gotten a full paycheck yet since I just started this job. Could you please send me enough to buy a dress for the party?"

"Ellen, I sent you some money last week," Hailey said with a trace of asperity. "What happened to that?"

"A measly hundred dollars?"

"That measly hundred dollars was hard to come by," Hailey said testily.

"I'm sorry, sis. I didn't mean to sound as though I'm not grateful. Gosh, I am! But I used that to buy a suit. You didn't expect me to start a new job without any decent clothes, did you?"

Hailey suspected that Ellen's closet was fairly bulging with "decent clothes." "I thought you said you needed that money for a deposit on a telephone."

"Well, I did. But I managed to borrow that from one of the girls I work with."

Hailey gnawed her bottom lip in vexation, but she put down her flash of temper and asked reasonably, "Do you think that's a good idea, Ellen? To borrow money from someone you've just met?"

"Oh, she didn't care. She's becoming one of my very best friends."

But for how long? Hailey wanted to ask. She rubbed her forehead, which had suddenly begun to pound. "Okay, Ellen, I'll send you a little more, but this is the last time." She recalled a pair of cold gray eyes glaring at her and remembered that she might not have a job herself.

"I understand," Ellen said solemnly, then burst forth with accolades to all of Hailey's virtues. "You're the best sister in the whole world, Hailey. I'm so lucky to have you to take care of me."

They said their good-byes, but it was a mechanical exercise for Hailey. Such scenes had happened too often in the past, and she admitted that they would probably happen again—in the near future. Breaking lifetime habits was difficult, if not impossible.

Ever since they were children, she had looked after Ellen. No one made a secret of the fact that Ellen was the "pretty one" and Hailey was the one with the brains. If Ellen was forgetful and irresponsible, she was forgiven because she looked so angelic. Their parents had never criticized her, nor rebuked her for letting her older sister do her thinking for her. Hailey had bailed Ellen out of numerous scrapes when they were children. Now, as adults, the pattern continued.

Hailey had always been burdened with a sense of responsibility. When her parents' health had failed toward the latter years of their lives, it was Hailey who stayed at home and took care of them. Ellen left home because she couldn't bear to be around sick people. Yet, it was she they yearned to see, to talk to. Hailey didn't really blame them. During Ellen's infrequent and hasty visits, the gloomy house would be filled with laughter and gaiety. Hailey's dependability was no match for Ellen's exuberance.

My God! Is this wallow in self-pity day? she asked herself as she flopped back against the pillows on her bed. What was wrong with her tonight? It was a rhetorical question that she already knew the answer to. What was wrong with her was Tyler Scott. She had built a life for herself, albeit a dull, colorless one. What would he do to that world?

As if on cue, the telephone rang again. Her hand

hovered above it, dreading to answer it, knowing instinctively who was calling. She was right.

"Miss Ashton," he said immediately after she said a low hello. "Tyler Scott."

"Yes, Mr. Scott. How is Faith?"

"Fine. I'm calling for another reason. I hope I didn't catch you at a bad time."

Was he serious? How could he pleasantly ask if it were a bad time when he was calling to fire her? "N . . . no. I was just lying down resting."

A significant pause yawned between them along the connecting cables. It was a silence that didn't need to be filled. It was already rife with innuendo. "Oh?" he asked on a lilting note. "I hope I didn't interrupt anything."

The insinuation was so bold, so blatant, so sexual that she sucked in her breath sharply. "No, Mr. Scott, you did not," she said firmly.

"My condolences. See me tomorrow at one o'clock in Sanders's office. Good night."

Outraged, she slammed down the phone. It had already gone dead in her hand. Damn him! How dare he infer anything about her personal life? And even if his sullied mind made such inferences, how dare he speak them out loud? She'd let him know in no uncertain terms what she thought of his seedy insinuations when she saw him.

Tomorrow.

What was he planning to do, to say? Why was he keeping her on pins and needles worrying about her job? Why didn't he take whatever action he planned to take and get it over with?

Forgoing the omelet, she stalked into her bathroom. She wouldn't have trouble finding another job. Not with her experience. Why should she care what he did? Let him fire her. Let him have his job. Could he do any better at it than she? "Not on your life, Mr. Scott," she shouted to the bathroom walls.

What she needed was a fling. Something unheard of. Even scandalous. She longed to do something totally unexpected and impulsive. Hailey Ashton had always been depended on to do the right thing, to behave properly. She always had, and she was sick of it. When had she ever disappointed, surprised, shocked anyone? Never. Such a thing would be good for her. What should it be? Rob a bank? Run naked through the streets? Have an affair?

Her head came up with a snap to look at her reflection in the mirror over the basin. Where had such an idea come from? She didn't know. Nor could she imagine what prompted the next thought that forced its way to the front of her mind. *I wonder what Tyler Scott thinks of me as a woman?*

Purely objectively, he *was* an exceedingly attractive man, if the strong, domineering type happened to appeal to you. His handsome features radiated raw masculinity, yet Hailey had seen a ghost of a smile when he talked about his insecurities as a parent. The steeliness of his eyes was intimidating, but they had softened and grown warm when he looked at Faith.

But the censorious looks he had leveled at her had hardly suggested barely contained lust! She laughed to herself. Of course, there was that brief moment when his eyes wandered in the vicinity of her breasts as he read her name tag, but that couldn't count. She had only imagined that it took an inordinate amount of time for him to read her name.

Then there was that small space of time that seemed to span infinity when he actually touched her, when his hard thumb evocatively embedded itself in the softness of her palm. Could he have detected the racing pulse in the wrist beneath his grasp?

Impatiently she switched off her bedside lamp, hoping that she might switch off the ridiculous conjectures that were flashing through her mind like an erotic slide show. Darkness didn't dispel them, however. Rather it seemed to intensify them as she tossed restlessly on her pillow. When at last she fell asleep, her body was still flushing hotly.

In her dreams it was she who was hurt and Tyler who did the tender healing. His touch was gentle, but electrifying. His eyes were sympathetic, but bold. His mouth . . .

She didn't sleep well at all.

The next morning was filled with its share of minor catastrophes. A wallet was lost and immediately found. Hailey was tearfully, gratefully thanked for her able assistance. Numerous lost children were quickly reunited with frantic parents. The infirmary reported one scraped knee and a sinus headache. Hailey personally greeted the senior citizen group that was going to have a catered picnic lunch on the grounds, see all the theater shows, and ride only the carousel. On behalf of the panicky social director, it was she who placed the call to the caterer, who was running an hour late but would be there shortly.

With all that activity, the morning should have passed quickly, but the hours dragged by with Hailey dreading her meeting with Tyler Scott more and more every minute.

At twelve-thirty she put Charlene in charge and left the office. The weather was still hot and humid, but she slipped a white blazer over her green uniform blouse. In any event, she would appear professional.

Harmon Sanders, general manager of the park, wasn't in his office, but his efficient secretary greeted Hailey as she walked into the carpeted office. It seemed far away from the clamorous noise of the amusement park. "Hi, Hailey."

"Hello, Nancy. Where is everyone?" Usually the office was crawling with department directors competing for a minute with the general manager.

"Everyone's lying low because of . . ." Her voice trailed off, but she indicated the closed door with an inclination of her head. "Him," she whispered. She crooked her finger at Hailey and leaned over the desk. "Can you believe that after three years, he suddenly decides to put in an appearance? Hailey, he's absolutely gorgeous! Wait till you see him! My God, I nearly died when he walked through that door and calmly introduced himself." She drew a deep breath, as though the memory of that moment still affected her.

"He asked me to send you in as soon as you arrived. Are you ready?" she asked with a compassion reserved for the hopelessly doomed.

"Yes," Hailey answered with more composure than she felt. She walked to the heavy walnut door and turned the brass knob. Tyler Scott was leaning over a wide desk, studying a computer readout that cluttered its glossy surface.

"Come in, Miss Ashton," he said, though he hadn't raised his head to confirm who had entered the room. How had he known it was she?

"Your Chanel precedes you," he answered as though he had read the question in her mind. He looked up at her from under the thick slash of eyebrows that bridged his forehead. "Sit down, please."

So his approach was to be friendly, not formal. He wouldn't have remarked on her perfume if he intended to be formal. When had he gotten close enough to her to know the fragrance she wore? How had he become so knowledgeable about perfume? Her knees were trembling as she went to one of two deep leather chairs in front of the desk and sat down, chastely crossing her legs and tugging on the hemline of her skirt.

His indignation over his rudeness on the telephone had been judiciously banked. What good would it do to antagonize him further? He was a cad, a chauvinist with a low opinion of women and a locker-room mentality. Nothing she would say could change that. It was far more prudent to ignore what he had said last night. She would keep the interview on a strictly professional basis.

A full minute went by before he rolled up the computer charts he was reading and sat down behind the desk. Strange that he hadn't assigned such a tedious task as going over statistics about Serendipity to a subordinate, but it was obvious that he had been working on them himself.

The cuffs of his starched white shirt were rolled up to his elbows. A pair of gold cuff links—with his initials in lower case—lay discarded on the desk. His striped tie had been loosened around his neck and the top button of his shirt was undone. The coat to his suit hung on a hall tree behind him, but he still wore the vest. Its snug fit accented his trim torso.

He leaned back in the chair, raised his feet onto the desk, and crossed one ankle over the other as he stared at her. "How are you, Miss Ashton?"

If he intended to confuse her, he was succeeding. She hadn't expected the casual civility. "I'm fine, thank you, Mr. Scott. How is Faith? Did the bee stings cause her any more pain?"

"No." He smiled. "Of course I've been banished from her bathroom, so I can't be certain, but I assume that all is well."

Hailey returned the smile and relaxed—but only a trifle. "Good. I've been worried about her. I would have called her this morning, but I didn't know where you were staying."

"At Glenstone Lodge. I've leased a suite of rooms there for the next several weeks."

That took her by surprise and it must have showed, for he continued. "My company is based in Atlanta. We have a home there, but I needed to come up here and do some revamping on the park. I also thought the change of scenery would be good for Faith. She hasn't been . . . comfortable . . . with me since her mother died."

"Shouldn't Faith be starting school in Atlanta?"

"Normally yes, but not this fall. Last spring after Monica's death, she began showing signs of stress. Her counselor thought it might be best to let her rest for a while. I've had her tutored this summer, but I don't think I'll enroll her in regular classes again until after Christmas. She should be able to catch up quickly enough since she's an 'A' student. I feel her emotional stability is more important than schoolwork just now."

"You're probably right." Why was he telling her all this? Not that she wasn't interested in the girl, who had seemed so eager to please her rather intimidating father. She had been touched by Faith's apparent insecurity. But it wasn't like a man as busy as Tyler Scott to divulge his family affairs to an employee he was about to fire.

"Do you like your work at Serendipity, Hailey?" he asked, changing the subject abruptly.

Had he called her Hailey? "Yes."

"You don't see any need to expound on that succinct answer?" There was a teasing glint in his gray eyes.

"Not really. I've been here for four years. I was here when the park was sold to you. Harmon . . . Mr. Sanders . . . has made it worth my while to stay. I've gotten periodic pay increases from him."

"From me, not Sanders."

"Oh," she floundered. "I'm sorry, I thought—"

"You thought that the man in Atlanta was too high up, too detached, to know each person in his employ? Not so with me, Hailey. I knew of you and your capabilities even before I purchased the park."

Capabilities? Would he say that if he were about to fire her?

"There was only one thing missing in my file on Miss Hailey Diane Ashton, twenty-eight years old, social security number 462-89-1002. Nowhere in the file did it say what a beautiful woman you are."

Her heart had long since leaped from her chest to settle somewhere in her throat. Now it began to pound, blocking off her breath. She tore her eyes away from the hypnotic allure of his gaze and concentrated on the hemline of her skirt.

When she braved another glance at him, he, too, was studying the hemline of her skirt, which revealed her smooth, nylon-clad knee. His eyes went further and took in her long, shapely calf and slender foot. She dared not move. Her head was spinning. What was he up to? Sexual harassment? Would she have to placate him to keep her job?

Etiquette forced her to respond. "Thank you," she said huskily.

"You're welcome," he said, standing up and walking around the desk to lean negligently on its corner. He sounded amused. Was he moving in for the kill?

"Have you ever thought of leaving Serendipity?"

She shook her head before she answered. "No. I like my job here."

"What if I offered you another job?"

He wasn't going to fire her! She looked up at him. "What kind of job?" she inquired curiously, though she doubted that she'd really be interested.

"I have a computer company. It needs someone like you in customer relations. I would like you to train my employees how to deal with people."

"But I don't know anything about computers!"

"You don't have to. You know about people. That's the expertise I'm looking for. Unfortunately some of my employees know every intricacy of a computer but have a difficult time relating to a customer—satisfied or irate. Would you consider it?"

She looked at him levelly for a moment and then down at her cold, damp hands. "I don't think so, Mr. Scott. I'm really very happy here at Serendipity."

"I see." He stared down at his highly polished shoes and frowned. The telephone in the outside office rang. They heard Nancy's muffled answer. Otherwise the heavy silence reigned in the air-conditioned room.

"I suppose you should continue in your present position then," he said, finally looking up at her. "Actually, your staying here will make it much more convenient."

"More convenient? Make what more convenient?"

"Your seduction," he said, piercing her with razor-sharp gray eyes..

CHAPTER 3

If he had suddenly sprouted wings, he couldn't have shocked her more. For long moments she couldn't speak, couldn't move. She could feel her mouth hanging slack in an expression usually attributed to the very stupid. *"What?"* she asked on an incredulous gasp.

"You heard me correctly."

"But I don't believe what I heard."

"I'm going to seduce you."

"Of course you're not serious."

"I'm always serious," he said. Then, as though to belie his own statement, he laughed a deep, masculine laugh, a pleasant sound she couldn't help but appreciate even though she was still stunned by his audacity.

"You seem surprised," he said. "Why? I think we'd make exceptional lovers. Our ages are compatible— I'm just a decade older than you. I can afford to give you anything you might want, but at the same time you don't have to depend on me for financial security. We're both well-educated and reasonably intelligent. My looks, to my knowledge, have never revolted anyone, and I've already told you that I think you're beautiful. We are ideally suited."

Furiously, Hailey sprang to her feet. She couldn't believe that a man, any man, would insult her so shamelessly. "I hope this is a joke, Mr. Scott," she flared.

"I assure you it is not. I intend to be your lover. Soon."

"I don't give a damn about your intentions except as to how they pertain to me professionally. I realize that I was rude to you the other day. I apologize. But I think your form of punishment is in the worst of taste. Your proposal flatters neither of us. Sexual harassment is the lowest form of abuse to a working woman. I'm not in the least bit interested in engaging in any kind of affair with you. If a simple 'no' doesn't discourage you, then you may put all your jobs in a hand basket and go straight to hell, Mr. Scott."

She spun on her heels and stormed toward the door. "Hailey," he said with such authority that she halted in spite of her haste to leave him. "Look at me." Not wanting him to think she was intimidated, she turned to face him again, haughty disdain exuding from every pore.

"Sexual harassment? I hadn't thought you'd take it like that but since you seem to be under that mistaken impression, I'll set you straight. You will not be harassed but persuaded."

"Semantics. It's the same thing."

He smiled. "Not quite. At least not the way *I* persuade. When we come together, you'll want me as badly as I want you."

"Don't hold your breath."

"I won't have to. You're already attracted to me."

"Oh!" she ground out through clenched teeth. "You're . . . I'm . . . I never—"

"You never thought for a moment that this was sexual harassment. Sexual harassment is an employer using an employee's job to blackmail him—or her. Your job is secure. Even if you weren't my employee, if we'd met under entirely different circumstances, I'd be just as determined to have you."

"But it doesn't hurt your depraved campaign that I happen to owe you a certain allegiance."

"You're a valuable employee. I wouldn't risk losing you to gratify a sudden explosion of lust. If I were the kind of man to do that, most likely, I would have already forced you into submission with threats against disclosure. And I wouldn't have wasted the past half hour talking, either.

"I was driven by panic yesterday. If any other guest had acted like that during an emergency, I would have expected my Director of Guest Relations to respond efficiently and expediently, just as you did. Your top priority was to take care of the distressed guest—in this case, Faith. You did exactly what you should have done."

She was momentarily disarmed by this flattery. "Thank you," she said stiffly.

"But," he stressed as he pushed himself away from

the desk and started toward her, "your being a competent employee has nothing to do with this."

He was within inches of her now, forcing her to tilt her head back to look at him. Her instinct for self-preservation screamed at her to run, but the fervor in his eyes compelled her to stay. His hands came up to settle on her shoulders. His mouth was perilously close to hers as he bent over her and whispered, "I want you in my life and I want you in my bed, Hailey."

She would have expected his mouth to be firm, hard, greedy, even brutal. But it was none of those. The lips that captured hers were soft and suppliant. He sipped at her lips, moving over them with infinite care, as though he feared she might disintegrate before he could drink his fill.

Hailey neither responded nor resisted. Shock had rendered her immobile. Yet with each heartbeat she felt her rigid control relaxing. Her lips parted as she felt his tongue gliding along them, slipping between them teasingly, but not breaching them completely. From far away she heard a small whimper and didn't even realize she had made the sound until her hands found their way to his waist where she sought support.

She swayed slightly and he caught her to him with a gentleness that was nonetheless ruthless. His arms wrapped around her like bands of steel—no, like velvet ribbons. In any event, she was powerless to escape them.

She made no conscious decision to open her lips to the persistent, tender probing of his tongue, but she did. Then he was inside her mouth, molding his lips with hers in a kiss that splintered her with pleasure.

She knew she should stop this. It was insane for her to stand there kissing this man, and it was also completely out of character. Yet only last night, in a moment of loneliness and depression, she had convinced herself she should do something wildly spontaneous, if for no other reason than for the sake of experience. Why not indulge that fantasy? She could stop it anytime. This was a harmless kiss. Nothing more.

Expertly and thoroughly, Tyler tasted, explored, and enjoyed her mouth. He drew from it secrets she hadn't known were harbored there. She moved closer to him, instinctively responding to the pressure of his tongue against hers.

A deep growl of desire went through the chest pressed so intimately against her breasts. Brazenly, she was thrilled that she—steady, dependable Hailey Ashton—could provoke such a reaction from this virile man.

At long last, breathless, he lifted his head and raked his scorching eyes over each feature of her face. His hands were sure and confident as he separated the lapels of her blazer. His gaze burned across her breasts. As though responding to his silent command, she felt her nipples tighten and strain against the fabric of her blouse.

He smiled tenderly. Strong, tanned fingers gently brushed back the copper curls from her flushed cheek. "When you know me better, I'll discover every delicious secret of your body, Hailey. You'll be all too willing to share them with me. I promise you that I'll know all of you from the inside out."

His softly spoken words broke the trance she had fallen into. She pushed away from him with such determination that he stumbled backward a few steps before he could regain his balance.

"You'll know nothing more of me than you already do, Mr. Scott." Her words were spoken in a low, strained voice. Never in her life had she been so furious with another human being. "I'm not going to let your bad manners and disgusting behavior frighten me away from a good job. I intend to continue working at Serendipity in the capacity I now hold. Should you unwisely decide to fire me or try to touch me again, I'll scream sexual harassment to the highest court in the land. You can't browbeat me into submission, either, so you may as well give up the effort and look for another, more obliging, victim."

The heel of her shoe made a dent in the lush carpet as she whirled around and slammed out the door. Nancy looked up anxiously. "That bad?" she asked worriedly.

Hailey swallowed the aspersions she would have liked to make about Mr. Tyler Scott and answered breezily, "Not at all. Mr. Scott and I understand each other perfectly." She left before Nancy could question her further.

By the time she reached her office, the soles of her feet were burning from the pounding she had given them on the hot asphalt. With each step, she had cursed Tyler Scott as the most arrogant, most conceited, most infuriating creature she had ever met.

His assumption that she wouldn't be able to resist him was incomprehensible. Did he think she was a weak specimen of the female sex, hungry for the touch of a man? Had he snickered over her employee file when he noted her age and marital status? Had he mentally dubbed her a frustrated old maid? Had he supposed that she was lonely enough and desperate enough for a man's attention that she would succumb to his advances without a quibble?

She instructed her assistant to carry on as she sailed through the outer office and into the tiny lavatory provided for her convenience. Her image in the mirror alarmed her. Had Charlene noticed her disarranged hair, moist lips, and flaming cheeks?

She was always immaculately groomed. Wouldn't everyone have seen that there was the slightest smudge of lipstick on her jaw? Tyler's lips had picked up the coral gloss from hers and carried it to that sensitive spot just under her ear. Luckily, her blazer hid the fact that her blouse was twisted and coming out of the waistband of her skirt.

Muttering self-deprecations, she quickly bathed her face with cold water and repaired her makeup. She brushed her hair and secured it into a tight prim knot on top of her head. Somewhat restored, she resolved to put the interlude out of her mind for the rest of the afternoon.

It wasn't so easy to do. Charlene noticed her supervisor's distraction immediately. "Say, Hailey, are you okay? I've asked you the same question three times. I get the impression you haven't heard a thing I've said."

"Yes, I'm fine," Hailey said. "I've got a headache, that's all."

"Well, what do you want me to tell him?"

"Tell who?"

"The high school principal from Knoxville," Charlene said wearily. "He wants to know about an end-of-season party for the football team."

"Oh, yes. When is the season over?"

"October thirtieth."

"Then why are you even bothering me with this? You know we close for the season on October first."

"Well, I just thought—"

"No exceptions, Charlene."

"All right, I'll tell him."

Hailey could tell by the girl's wounded tone that she had been unfairly using her as a scapegoat for her own bad temper. "I'm sorry, Charlene," she said by way of conciliation. "If you'll give me his number, I'll call him myself. And I apologize for being so grouchy. It's been a rough day."

"That's okay. I think it's the humidity."

In Hailey's case, it wasn't the humidity. It was a pair of gray eyes, flecked with ebony and fringed with spiky black lashes, that kept interfering with her work and souring her disposition. It was the vivid recollection of urgent lips demanding a response in the gentlest of ways. It was a hard, taut body pressed against hers, acquainting her with the male physique in a way that left her trembling.

She hadn't known many men, had certainly never been deeply involved with any. Now this man was storming his way into her life with plans to use her just as everyone else had. What was it about her that made people think they could take advantage? Was she too dependable? Too acquiescent? Or was cowardly a better word?

All her life she had been used. By her parents to set a good example for Ellen. By Ellen to do her dirty work and get her out of trouble. By friends to whom she could never refuse a favor even at her own expense. She had learned the hard way that people are avaricious and grasping and that it was human nature to take advantage of one who was weak.

But maturity, repeated disillusionment, and heartache had taught Hailey well. She had achieved independence and guarded it fiercely. She'd be no one's doormat. Not Tyler Scott's. Not anyone's.

Eight o'clock found her checking over the tally of guests who had walked through the turnstiles that day. At the sound of her name, she raised her head and looked through the plate-glass windows that enclosed her office to see Faith Scott charging around the fountain outside. The girl was out of breath, her broadly smiling face bathed with a film of healthy perspiration, when she came to an abrupt halt on the other side of the glass and cried, "Isn't it great, Hailey?"

Hailey slid the window open so they could hear each other without shouting. She was laughing at the sheer delight written all over Faith's features. "Isn't what great?"

"Daddy told me you're coming to dinner with us."

Indeed, Tyler looked quite pleased with himself as he sauntered around the pool of water surrounding the fountain. His coat was negligently hitched over his shoulder by an index finger. His long stride brought him quickly up to the window, where he casually draped his arm around Faith's shoulders. "Hi," he said.

Hailey wanted to scream. His taunting grin was more irritating than his seductive promises had been. She was on the verge of telling him that she wasn't at his beck and call when she happened to glance down into Faith's expectant face. The harsh words died an instant death on her lips. Tyler was using the child for his own devious ends. But Faith was innocent, and Hailey didn't want the girl's disappointment to be on her conscience.

"How are the bee stings?" she asked Faith, ignoring Tyler.

"No sweat. Daddy got that stuff you told him to get at the drugstore and by this morning they didn't hurt at all. You sure are smart."

"I'm just glad I outsmarted the bee."

Faith giggled. "Are you ready to go?"

Hailey looked up at Tyler for the first time and

smiled sweetly. She was satisfied to see that her con-
geniality surprised him. "I'll be just a minute."

She went into her office to get her blazer and purse.
On her way out, she issued last-minute instructions to
Charlene, who would be responsible for the office until
the park closed at ten o'clock. She left by a back door
after checking her appearance in the lavatory mirror.
She swore to herself that it didn't matter what she
looked like—she wasn't trying to impress anyone, especially Tyler Scott.

Faith was waiting eagerly. Tyler was lounging with
one foot braced on a park bench as though he had
never given a thought to the possibility that she might
refuse the dinner invitation.

"My car is—"

"We'll walk you to it and follow you home. We'll
even wait if you want to change, won't we Faith?"

"Yeah. I want to see where you live, Hailey."

Damn! He had outmaneuvered her again by involv-
ing Faith. Hailey had planned to drive her own car to
wherever he chose to eat so he wouldn't learn where
she lived. Of course, all he had to do was check her file
to find her address. Still, it rankled that he had scored
the point so easily.

"I live in a duplex up on the mountain, Faith," Hailey said, deliberately excluding Tyler from the conversation. "I lease out the other side of my house to
tourists. In the winter there are hordes of skiers looking for lodging."

"That's dangerous, isn't it?" Tyler asked, casually

taking her arm as they crossed an intersection in the employees' parking lot. "Having strangers under your roof."

"I'm very careful about whom I lease to."

"But for a woman living alone, I would think—"

"I never said that I live alone."

He halted so abruptly that the fingers around her elbow bit into her skin. "You do, don't you?"

The fierceness of his expression alarmed her. His brows had drawn together over his piercing eyes in what could only be called a scowl. His lips were pressed into a grim line. Her newfound independence hadn't replaced caution. She didn't dare reply flippantly.

"Yes, I do," she said calmly. Then she added under her breath for his ears alone, "Not that it's any of your damn business who I live with."

"I'm making it my business. I'm a possessive, selfish lover, Hailey. I'll share you with no one."

She opened her mouth, ready to set him straight on both points, but Faith's piping voice asked, "Which car is yours, Hailey?"

Hailey shook her head, trying to clear it. Things were happening too fast and she couldn't handle them. She wanted to tell this overbearing brute that his possessive attitude was ridiculous, but there seemed to be no opportunity.

"Its . . . uh . . . there. The blue Jeep."

"A Jeep! Oh, neat!" Faith cried and raced toward the

parked car. "Can I ride with you, Hailey? Can I, Daddy? Please?"

"I think you should be asking Hailey, not me."

Faith turned pleading eyes on her, and they were too much to resist. "Of course you may, but I must warn you that anyone riding in my car has to use a seat belt."

"That's okay. My daddy makes me use one, too."

Hailey unlocked the passenger door, then came around to unlock hers. Tyler placed a hand on her shoulder and said, "My car is parked back there." He made a motion with his head. "Wait for me at the gate. I'll follow you." It wasn't a request. It was a polite command that told her not to even think about leaving the parking lot without him behind her.

To soften the order, his fingers caressed her shoulder, and in the next instant, his mouth swooped down on hers to deliver a hard, quick kiss on her surprised mouth. Her cheeks flamed and she was immensely glad that Faith had already climbed into the car and hadn't seen what had happened. Rebuking him for the kiss would only bring the girl's attention to them.

Hailey turned away from him and fumbled with the door handle. One glance told her Tyler was making his way to his own car.

"We'll leave the windows open until some of this hot air blows out, then I'll turn on the air conditioner. It's not really practical for a Jeep to have an air conditioner, but I was spoiled." Hailey smiled down into the face that was looking up at her adoringly.

"I think it's terrific, but why did you get a jeep?" Faith asked with the unrestrained curiosity of a child.

Hailey laughed. "You'll see why on the way home."

Gatlinburg was a small tourist town dedicated to preserving its quaintness, and the streets were narrow and congested with traffic. She avoided Parkway, which was the main thoroughfare through the center of town, and took the road that ran beside the fast flowing Little Pigeon River. She turned right onto one of the roads leading up the side of the mountain. The jeep took the intricate twists and turns of the winding road with ease. Hailey was disgruntled to see that the large, powerful Lincoln, which had actually beaten them to the exit gate of the parking lot, did almost as well.

Her duplex was literally perched on the side of the mountain. Faith scrambled out of the jeep when Hailey pulled it to a stop on her small expanse of driveway. "Be careful," Hailey cautioned as she followed at a more sedate pace. She didn't even look to see if Tyler was behind them. She assumed correctly that he was.

"I will. Oh, gee, this is super. Which part do you live in?"

"The upper story."

"Is anyone in the lower one?"

"Not now, no."

The structure was a study of wood shingles, glass, and odd angles. The roof was drastically pitched. Redwood decking provided Hailey with a front porch that seemed suspended in mid-air with no visible means of support. It provided a spectacular view of Gatlinburg nestled in the floor of the valley far below.

She unlocked the front door, and Faith dashed uninhibitedly inside. Hailey bent down to pick up the evening paper lying near the front door.

"Very nice." The voice was low, intimate, and stirring.

She straightened and turned around to face Tyler. He wasn't looking at the view, or even her house. He had been looking at her as she bent over to retrieve her paper. "Thank you," she said with barely contained anger.

"You're mad at me, aren't you?"

"Disgusted is a more appropriate word."

"Why?"

"Because I didn't think even a man like you would use his own daughter for procurement."

The insult did what she hoped it would. It destroyed the insolent triumphant expression on his tanned face and changed it to one of anger. Before he had a chance to either defend himself or counterattack, Faith demanded from the doorway, "Aren't you two coming in?"

"Right now!" Hailey said with false gaiety, whirling so that her skirt swung out saucily. "Make yourself at home, Mr. Scott. There are cold drinks in the refrigerator for you and Faith."

"I'd rather come with you," Faith said. She had already peeked into Hailey's bedroom and apparently found it completely intriguing.

"Okay, you can pick out something for me to wear."

"Really?" Faith asked before charging toward the bedroom.

By the time Hailey got to the room, Faith was already rifling through the contents of her closet. "This," she said, taking out a sundress that still had the price tag hanging from it.

"Oh, I don't know," Hailey demurred. She had bought the dress on impulse at the beginning of the summer and had yet to wear it. The right occasion had never arisen, and the dress showed more skin than she usually felt comfortable displaying. Ellen had begged her for the dress, but she had refused to give it to her. Why, she didn't know. For some reason having such a dress in her closet made it seem possible that something exciting might happen in her otherwise dreary life.

"It's beautiful," Faith said.

"Chic" was a more suitable adjective than beautiful. Made of denim and trimmed in white eyelet, its dropped waistline permitted the full skirt to flare at just the right spot on the hips. A border of eyelet petticoat peeked from beneath a deep ruffle on the bottom of the midcalf-length skirt. The bodice was fitted tightly, and since it was held up only by spaghetti-thin straps, it required either a strapless bra or none at all. Hailey didn't have a strapless bra.

"Well . . ."

"Come on, Hailey. Please wear it."

Fearing that she would hurt Faith's feelings if she

didn't, she conceded. It was silly not to wear it, after all. The season was almost over, and if she didn't wear it now, she might not get a chance. Next summer, it would probably be out of style. Even though it was bare and she wouldn't be wearing all that much underneath it, she wasn't wearing it to enchant Mr. Scott, she told herself. If he misinterpreted her motives, he'd find out just how wrong he was.

While Faith kept up a steady stream of chatter, Hailey changed in the connecting bathroom. The dress fit her trim figure to perfection, clinging to her breasts like a second skin. She put her hair back up with decorative combs after thoroughly brushing it.

Faith's curiosity overrode her manners, and she tapped lightly on the bathroom door. "Can I come in?"

"Sure," Hailey answered. Faith watched in fascination while Hailey applied fresh makeup. She was nosy and curious and meddlesome, but endearing. Apparently, Faith was eager for a woman's opinion of her own appearance and missed having her mother to talk to about such things.

Hailey asked for her help in selecting a flat, strappy sandal to wear with the sundress. After Hailey had misted herself with Chanel, she sprayed some on Faith. The girl's expression was one of rapture, and Hailey found it pitifully touching that so small a gesture could mean so much to the girl.

Of one thing Hailey was certain, the child adored her father. "Daddy said," "Daddy thinks," "Daddy is,"—these expressions prefaced most of her sentences. It was clear to Hailey that Faith held him in awe. Her desire for his acceptance and approval was pathetic.

When Hailey was ready, they went into the living room where Tyler was a dark silhouette against the violet of dusk at the window. When he heard them, he turned around. His eyes opened wide in unconcealed appreciation of Hailey's efforts.

Hailey had to put down an urge to cover the expanse of bare skin on her shoulders and chest. "I think we're ready," she said. The timidity in her voice was humiliating. She sounded like a girl going out on her first date.

"Your home is lovely," Tyler said. Hailey's eyes swept the room as though seeing it for the first time. A stone fireplace took up one wall, while plate-glass windows took up another. The sofa and chairs were covered in a nubby, cream-colored fabric and piled with cushions of contrasting earth tones. Area rugs relieved the bareness of the parquet oak floor. Louvered barroom doors led into the kitchen, and the far end of the living room had been made into a dining alcove.

"If you think this room is pretty, you ought to see her bedroom. She's got a bedspread in a peachy color and it's so soft. And the bathroom is yummy. There's this sunken bathtub, and it's the same color as the bedspread. You ought to see it, Daddy."

His gray eyes swung to Hailey and she dropped hers in mortification. "Maybe I will sometime," he said in a seductive tone. "Where did you say you wanted to eat,

Faith?" He wasn't looking at his daughter. His eyes remained riveted on Hailey.

"It's really neat," Faith said in what she hoped was a selling voice. "They've got pizza and lasagna and electronic games in the back room."

That got Tyler's attention and he laughed indulgently. "My child is addicted to those computerized games," he said to Hailey.

She smiled back. "I think everyone is these days."

"Do you mind a restaurant with electronic games in the back room?" His look was rueful and apologetic.

"Of course not. I may even try them myself."

"Great! Let's go. I'm starving." Faith dragged out the last word dramatically and they all laughed.

Hailey locked her house and she and Tyler followed Faith up the steps to his car. He placed a proprietary arm around her shoulders and drew her closer to him.

"I may have to change your uniform at Serendipity. You look gorgeous tonight, Hailey."

The breath that fanned her cheek was fragrant and minty and caused a ridiculous fluttering in her throat. Her "thank you" sounded thoroughly unnatural.

"I like you with more skin and less underwear."

His candid remark changed her timorousness to fury. She pushed away from him. "You can't talk to me like that," she said heatedly.

His teeth shone whitely through the darkness as his smile widened. "Sure I can. I'm going to be your lover, remember?" She began sputtering a scathing comeback, but he interrupted it. "Save those arguments for later when I will gladly prove each one futile. Right now Faith's waiting for us."

She resisted the arm he replaced across her shoulders, but when they reached the car, it was still there. She hadn't been able to break his hold on her.

The restaurant Faith had chosen was as noisy and crowded as Tyler had predicted it would be. A five-dollar bill slipped into the hand of the senior waiter shortened their wait and secured them a table near the windows overlooking the busy sidewalk and as far away from the whirring and zinging sounds emanating from the back room. Once Faith had ordered, she went to check out the games and came back to report that they were the "absolutely neatest" games available.

The salads had too much dressing and the lettuce had been allowed to wilt, but the lasagna was hearty and delicious. The Chianti, which Tyler had insisted Hailey share with him, was cold and potent and dangerous, since she was already suffering from lightheadedness. Much as she didn't want to admit it, Tyler Scott had a profound effect on her senses.

She could find no fault with either his manners or his conversation. He was devastatingly handsome, a fact which every other woman in the room had noted, Hailey realized glumly. He had taken off his suit coat and vest because of the heat, and his trim frame looked harder and more powerful than ever. His rolled-back shirt sleeves showed sinewy forearms sprinkled with dark hair. The fabric of his shirt, stretched across the sculpted muscles of his chest, revealed only a shadowy suggestion of the masculinity that lay beneath it.

When his eyes met hers across the red-and-white-checked tablecloth, Hailey's heart pounded so hard it frightened her. Had she read a description of such feelings in a novel, she would have scoffed and thought them to be the fanciful imaginings of the fiction writer. But these fingers of sensation that danced around her breasts, tautened her nipples, and curled downward to become that delightful weightiness in the pit of her stomach were all too real, all too disturbing.

With a mouthful of lasagna, Faith said, "I wish I could be beautiful like you, Hailey. Don't you think she's beautiful, Daddy?"

Hailey was saved from meeting his appraising gray stare because she immediately choked on her wine. She coughed into her napkin and gulped for air. When she did raise her watering eyes to meet his gaze, his eyes were twinkling with humor.

"She's very beautiful."

Hailey dabbed at the tears in her eyes. "No, I'm not beautiful, Faith. My sister Ellen is the pretty one in my family."

"You're so beautiful! I'll never be pretty because my daddy makes me wear these dumb glasses. He says

I'm too young for contact lenses." She cast her father an accusatory glare. "What do you think, Hailey?"

Hailey pretended to scrutinize the girl, though she wasn't about to contradict Tyler on the point. "I'll tell you what my parents did. They let me get contact lenses when my braces came off. Sort of a celebration present."

Faith's eyes behind her hated eyeglasses were as wide as her disbelieving mouth. "You wore *braces*?"

"A whole mouthful of them for three years," Hailey said, laughing.

"And you had to wear glasses, too?"

"Until I got contacts. And I still wear my glasses occasionally when my eyes are tired."

"But I bet you don't look dumb in them like I do."

"You don't look dumb at all. I think glasses look chic. Do you realize how many celebrities have started wearing them? Jane Fonda wears them. Robert Redford, Warren Beatty."

"Gee," Faith said. She stared into her empty plate as she contemplated what Hailey had said.

Hailey glanced at Tyler. His expression was soft, a half-smile, private. Lifting his wineglass, his eyes asked her to do the same. He mouthed the words "thank you" as he clinked his glass with hers. Then their eyes locked over the raised wineglasses. Hailey could no more draw her eyes from his gaze than she could move her little finger from the scarcely perceptible caressing of his.

Emotion squeezed her throat. A hot flush crept up

her neck and suffused her earlobes with throbbing heat. The pad of his little finger rubbed against hers, and she felt an electric current racing up her arm and into her breasts, making them tingle with excitement.

"Can I go play now?"

Hailey jumped at the intrusion of Faith's voice. She had become oblivious to everything in the room except the man whose stare was mesmerizing her. Perhaps she could have fought the magnetism of his eyes, but combined with the feel of his skin against hers, it left her defenseless.

"*May* I be excused and *may* I go play," Tyler corrected, forcibly breaking his eye contact with Hailey and lowering his glass to the table.

Faith sighed with adolescent exaggeration. "*May* I be excused and *may* I go play? Please?"

Tyler smiled. "You may. Here are two dollars," he said, fishing the bills out of his pocket "Get them changed at the cash register and be careful how you spend them."

"Thanks, Daddy. I'll make them last," Faith promised as she grabbed the money, took one last slurping drink of her Coke, and bolted from the table.

Hailey had used the time to regain her slipping control. What was wrong with her? She felt as faint and flustered as a maiden aunt with the vapors. It was lunacy to be swayed by a man like Tyler Scott. He was a taker, a user, accustomed to having his way. His technique was polished. He knew exactly how to play upon a woman's emotions. No doubt he had had plenty of practice applying his charm, but Hailey Ashton had had little practice fending it off.

Schooling her features to show no emotion, she sat up straighter in her chair, smoothed her hair, licked her lips, and tried to give off an air of cool composure. From experience she knew that if she gave him an inch, he'd take . . .

"Coffee?" he asked.

"Yes, please," she said tersely.

While they were waiting for the coffee to be delivered, she feigned absorption in the parade of foot traffic on the sidewalk, though in truth she saw nothing. He didn't try to engage her in conversation, but she could feel his eyes, touching her everywhere, seeing everything. Again she had an insane compulsion to cover herself.

"Cream?" He brought her eyes around to him.

"Yes, please."

"Say when." He poured the cream into her cup until she gave him the word.

"Thank you."

"You're welcome," he replied with mocking politeness.

She sipped her coffee, refusing to look at him. He was stirring his own absently. "You don't have to be this way, you know," he said quietly.

"What way?" Her defenses were up.

"All uptight, on guard, wary. I'm not going to rip your clothes off and ravage you on top of the table."

His mouth slanted into a wicked grin and a lid dropped over one eye. "At least not the first time."

"Mr. Scott—"

"Okay, okay, I'm sorry. You're so damned jumpy. Can't you take a joke?"

"I didn't think it was funny."

"Then I'll work on finding something to amuse you."

She dropped her eyes in embarrassment. Suddenly she felt very young and very foolish. "I usually have a keen sense of humor, but you've put me on the defensive because of . . . of what happened this afternoon and . . ."

"And?"

"And the things you've said."

When he didn't respond, she raised cautious eyes. He was pondering her quietly. "When I want something I tend to go after it, full steam ahead and damn the torpedoes. I apologize, Hailey. I want you. You know that. But I've rushed you and I didn't realize until now how impatient I've been or how crass I must seem to you. I promise to slow down, to give you breathing room."

At that moment she felt her last defensive wall crumbling. The mellow glow in his eyes and the dulcet tone of his voice conquered her will as force never could have.

"Tell me about yourself," he said quietly. "About your life prior to meeting me. You mentioned a sister. Does she live here?"

"No, in Nashville. She works for a recording company."

"Doing what?"

"Clerical work."

"Has she gone as far in her career as you have in yours?"

Hailey laughed softly. "I don't mean to be unkind, but no, she hasn't. She more than makes up for lack of brains, though. She's very beautiful."

"So you said before. 'Ellen is the pretty one in my family.' I'll take issue with that later. What about your parents?"

"They're not alive. I grew up in Knoxville. Both my parents became ill shortly after I graduated from college and began working as a service representative for the telephone company. I lived with them and took care of them. They died within months of each other. I sold the house, applied for the job at Serendipity, and here I am. Not very exciting."

"You excite me."

She had been staring pensively into space, but her eyes flew to his at his softly, seriously spoken words. The fire she saw smoldering in the gray depths gave credence to his statement.

"But to prove to you that I'm not the villain you've colored me to be, I'll tell you more than you want to know about myself."

He took a sip of coffee, asked the waiter to refill both their cups, glanced over his shoulder to see that

Faith was safely engrossed in one of her games, and then spoke again.

"I led a very privileged youth. Prep school. Harvard business school. I was expected to marry well and I did. It would be difficult to determine who caused whom the most misery. Monica and I never had more than an affectionate tolerance for each other. After a year and a half, we were divorced.

"Faith was the only good thing to come out of the marriage. Since in those days it was rarely contested to whom the child should go, Monica reared our daughter. I devoted my life to building my father's big conglomerate into a bigger one. When Monica was killed, Faith and I, who were only acquainted by short, hectic, weekend visits, were suddenly thrown together. We're still feeling our way with each other." He sighed heavily. "So there you have it—the life and loves of Tyler Scott."

Hailey couldn't feel sorry for someone who had grown up with every opportunity money can buy, yet hadn't been happy even then. She asked the first question that came into her mind. "What was Monica like?"

"Physically? Blonde, beautiful."

She suppressed a sharp stab of jealousy and asked, "Was she a good mother?"

"I can't criticize her, because I played such an inactive role in Faith's upbringing. She was as good a mother as an active tennis player, bridge player, social butterfly can be. I think Faith measured herself against her mother's poise and found herself wanting. I doubt if Monica ever realized Faith's inferiority complex or if she ever reassured her as you did tonight. Thank you for that."

"I know how it hurts to feel unattractive."

"Speaking from experience?"

"Yes. Compared to the way I was in my adolescence, Faith has the grace of a prima ballerina. Glasses, braces, red hair, tall, skinny. I was the perfect model for a 'before' picture in a complete make-over program."

Tyler propped his elbows on the table and leaned across it to whisper confidentially, "Miss Ashton, have you looked in a mirror lately?"

The question and the intensity with which he had asked it puzzled her. Before she could decipher his meaning, Faith came bounding up to the table and exclaimed, "I've done Space Invaders, Frogger, and Pac Man. Will you come play with me now? Pl-eee-ze."

"How could we refuse an invitation like that? Hailey, are you game?"

"Lead on," she said, rising gracefully from her chair only to have Faith grab her by the hand and drag her toward the back room.

For the next half hour Tyler fed the game machines with quarters. The adults were chagrined that Faith was far more adept at playing than they, but they all enjoyed the laughing and shouting that went with plying their skills. When a group of teenage boys became rowdy and their language too explicit for Faith's ears,

Tyler quickly hustled them out, bribing his daughter with the promise of an ice cream cone.

"Do you know Sweethearts Ice Cream Parlor in the Village?" he asked Hailey.

"They have peaches 'n' cream. That's my favorite," Faith piped up.

"Sure I know Sweethearts. But I'm in a rut. I can't break myself of the chocolate-chip habit."

They bantered jovially as they strolled the sidewalk, which was still thronged with tourists. The curio and souvenir shops were busy with shoppers. Children and adults alike indulged themselves with candy from the numerous candy kitchens, lemonade from sidewalk stands, or fresh doughnuts. For those in need of a rest, one of the larger souvenir shops had provided rocking chairs at the storefront. Shoppers could sit and enjoy the sights and sounds without exerting themselves.

Architecturally the Village mall resembled a Bavarian township. The shops were quaint and diverse, featuring everything from Waterford crystal to kosher dill pickles to unique Christmas ornaments.

At this time of evening, Sweethearts was a popular spot, and it took time to decide on a flavor from the large variety on the menu. Tyler, Hailey, and Faith were forced to stand in line. Normally Hailey enjoyed the ice cream parlor with its red, flocked wallpaper and collection of Coca-Cola memorabilia. But tonight she was suffering from an agony both rare and wonderful.

Since they had left the restaurant, Tyler had kept a possessive hand around the back of her neck. His touch was light, his fingers caressing, and she didn't doubt for a moment that he knew about the warmth he was spreading through her.

Now, as they were standing in the waiting line and he was discussing the merits of plain vanilla with Faith, his hand slipped down the bare skin of her back. With his index finger he distractedly traced the eyelet border of her bodice from one side of her back to the other. A now familiar lethargy crept into her limbs and she felt herself relying on the support of his tall, strong body beside her.

His fingers curved around her throat and his thumb tilted her head back as he leaned over her. "What do *you* think?"

She couldn't think at all. Her thoughts were all centered around him—how perfectly male he was, how she would love to touch his hair, how his brows were wiry, and how her fingers longed for the chance to smooth them. His slender nose and curving mouth were faintly reminiscent of ancient Greek sculpture.

She didn't realize how vulnerable, how feminine, she looked as she gazed up at him. The ceiling fans circling lazily overhead gently disarranged the wisps of hair lying against her cheeks and forehead. Her throat was arched, the pulse beating in it visibly agitated. Her green eyes were filled with an unintentionally seductive appeal.

The relevance of his question eluded her, but she said, "I'll stick to my chocolate chip."

His eyes lowered significantly to her mouth, which

was parted and tremulous as rapid little breaths escaped from it. "Can I taste it?"

He wasn't referring to the ice cream, and they both knew it. The conversation—not to mention the situation—was getting out of hand. Hailey knew she was sinking into a pool of desire that would surely drown her if she didn't save herself now. She eased away from his possessive touch. *"May* I taste it."

Faith thought Hailey's correcting her father, as he had corrected her, extremely funny, and she dissolved into a fit of giggles that outlasted the ice cream cones.

"It's home to bed for you, Faith, my girl," Tyler said as he ushered them out of the Village and toward the parked Lincoln. Faith climbed into the backseat without being told to, taking it for granted that Hailey would ride in the front with Tyler. "I'm going to drop you off at the Glenstone, ask Harry to see you to the suite, and then I'll take Hailey home."

"Can . . . may I at least go swimming?"

"Not unless I'm there to watch you. Besides, the pool closes at ten. But we'll go in the morning if you're fast asleep when I get home."

"Okay," Faith grumbled. As Hailey turned around to commiserate, Faith was stifling a broad yawn. Tyler had seen it in the rearview mirror and they smiled conspiratorially.

The night manager at the Glenstone promised to see Faith safely to the Scotts' suite. The girl blew Hailey a kiss as she and Tyler left through the massive glass doors at the front of the hotel. Hailey threw her a kiss back.

"She'd deny she was sleepy to the bitter end," Tyler said, chuckling as he engaged the gears of the car and steered it out onto the street.

"That's a universal trait of all children."

"Do you know much about children, Hailey?"

"No. I have only my childhood to base my theories on."

"I'll admit that I've never found a job harder than that of parenting. It baffles me."

"In what respect?" she asked slowly. She'd never come right out and tell him that his own daughter was unsure of his love. A man of Tyler Scott's pride couldn't handle criticism like that. It would be better to let him talk and perhaps learn from him the areas where he was lacking in understanding.

He laughed mirthlessly at her question. "In just about every respect. I don't think I appreciated the complexities of the female mind until I was forced to cope with an eleven-year-old girl."

"Faith is trying just as hard to cope with herself. A girl her age doesn't like herself very much. She wants to be a woman, but the idea frightens her. Her body is maturing at a rate that her psyche can't keep up with."

"Like getting stung on the breast by a bee and being too embarrassed to tell her father about it."

Hailey smiled tenderly. "Yes. She's extremely sensitive and reveals only a fraction of what she feels. More than anything, she wants you to be proud of her."

He swung his head to her. "I *am* proud of her."

Hailey was tempted to ask him if he had told Faith that but didn't think it was her place to interfere. Instead, she said, "She's a wonderful girl and promises to be a lovely young woman."

He laughed. "And she finds you equally wonderful. Ever since you helped her yesterday, all I've heard is Hailey this and Hailey that."

She laughed back. "All I hear about is you."

"Oh no," he groaned. "Has she told you about any of my bad habits?"

"Like what?"

"Like the blasphemous language I'm apt to use on the golf course."

"How many times have you and Faith played golf together?"

He pulled the car to a stop in her driveway and grinned at her. "I see your point. She doesn't know about that nasty habit. Maybe I'll be able to hide the others from her."

"What others?"

"No, no. I only divulge my bad habits one at a time."

Their soft laughter filled the confines of the car, but it was shatteringly interrupted by a brilliant streak of lightning and a resultant clap of thunder. Almost instantly the windshield was peppered with raindrops.

"Whew," Tyler said. "I guess this is what the heat and humidity have been building to."

"I guess so," Hailey murmured. Suddenly the atmosphere in the car was as electric as the storm outside. The air was too thick to breathe. The sudden flashes of lightning only punctuated the intervals of darkness. The small sounds inside the car were magnified in the silence following each crack of thunder.

Hailey's heart was pounding with awareness of the man an arm's-reach away. Intuitively, she knew he was just as aware of her. The awareness became suffocating, like a blanket that had been wrapped around them.

"Thank you for the evening," Hailey said hastily and reached for the door handle.

His hand shot across the velour-covered seat with uncanny speed and startling accuracy to clamp her wrist. "I've never failed to escort a lady to her door, Miss Ashton. Particularly during a thunderstorm. Stay put."

He was out of his door and opening hers before she could come to grips with the situation and formulate a plan of resistance in her mind. With the sure guidance of his hand on the small of her back, she ducked her head against the rain and ran for the protective covering over the redwood deck.

"My key . . ." She fumbled through the contents of her handbag, trying vainly to find the key. When at last her clumsy fingers closed around it she turned to Tyler and said, "Good night."

A hasty retreat was too much to hope for. Before she could get the key in the lock, Tyler had managed to back her against the wall, cutting off any means of escape by planting his palms on either side of her head.

Her breath was short and shallow from her recent run and his nearness, but she tried to speak with strong conviction when she said, "Mr. Scott, we've already played this scene once today, and I'm growing tired of it. I told you then and I'll tell you now—"

"Be quiet."

He delayed no further, but claimed her mouth with his. What little restraint he had placed on himself in his office had diminished throughout the day until now it was nonexistent. No longer tentative, no longer hesitant, no longer patient, he countenanced no resistance.

His lips opened over hers and it became impossible for her to remain passive. Every cell in her body surged to life. Her skin tingled with a strange, new excitement as his hands settled on her arms and crept upward in a sensuous ascent. He caressed her shoulders before moving his hands again to form a cradle for her face.

Keeping her head immobile with the merest pressure of his palms, his mouth coaxed hers to participate. "Don't hold anything back, Hailey," he said against her lips.

Knowing she was out of her league, but wanting desperately to learn the game, she parted her lips and accepted the heat of his mouth.

His tongue became a torch that inflamed her. It dipped into her mouth, darting at will until she closed her lips around it, turning the tables and making him the prisoner.

His groan echoed the deep, rumbling thunder that

bounced off the hillsides. He pulled his mouth free of hers only to explore the soft skin under her ear. Her hair spilled over his hands when his deft fingers released it from the combs that held it up.

"Hailey, Hailey," he whispered urgently. "You still see yourself as that bespectacled, awkward, skinny teenager in braces, don't you? Can't you see what a desirable woman you are?"

"Tyler . . . Mr. Scott . . ."

"Tyler."

"Tyler, please . . . I don't want you to do this."

"Yes you do."

Yes, she did. His mouth nibbled kisses along her collarbone. She felt her will dissolving as surely as her muscles seemed to be, and she put her arms around his neck for support. She gave in to a whim that had plagued her since she first saw him, and she touched the dark hair that curled against his collar and the wings of silver at his temples.

She never quite remembered when he lowered the thin straps of her dress, but she never forgot the moment his fingers began stroking the fevered skin of her chest. "I knew you'd feel like this. Warm satin. If fantasies were real, I would have already loved you a hundred times, Hailey. Loved you in every way a man can love a woman, and invented new ways."

The love words he whispered were outrageous when she applied them to herself. Nevertheless, they were transporting. What if they were only what every woman wanted to hear? What if he had learned them from long and frequent use? What if they would be forgotten and meaningless by tomorrow? For now they were a little bit crazy and very, very thrilling to hear. Were these words for her? For Hailey Ashton, known only to men as a pleasant companion, a competent co-worker, but never as a lover?

His lips deserted the hollow of her shoulder to come back to her mouth. Their mouths and noses nuzzled in sweet restraint until simultaneously they ceased to play and kissed each other hungrily.

His hands drew hers from around his neck and lowered them to his waist. Without modesty, she wrapped her arms around him, wanting to feel the muscles she knew now only as rippling curves under his shirt. Her fingers marveled at the hard compactness of his body. The rain that had moistened his face had released the scent of his cologne, and the fragrance, combined with his own essence, intoxicated her.

"Hailey?"

"Hm?"

He lifted one of her hands again. Turning his head, he pressed his lips into her soft palm. "Tyler," she gasped softly when she felt the wet heat of his tongue against the tender flesh.

"Hailey, let's touch each other." She wasn't thinking quickly enough to grasp his meaning before he slipped her hand between the buttons of his shirt and pressed it against his warm, hair-matted skin. The feel of him against her fingertips momentarily robbed her of consciousness. She didn't realize he had unbuttoned the first button on her already low bodice, and was skimming his fingers across the fullness of her breasts, until it was too late to resist.

The protest she had formed in her mind changed character before it left her throat and became nothing more than sighing acquiescence by the time it escaped her lips. His hands responded. The straps already lying on her arms were lowered another degree and the fabric so tenuously protecting her fell away under his questing fingers.

She was enclosed in the warm security of his hands. She filled them generously, but not heavily. He appreciated the firm ripeness before allowing his thumbs to test the delicate tips for their response. He wasn't disappointed. They pouted beneath his inquisitive touch.

"Oh, no." Hailey, swamped by a mounting desire she had never known could exist outside the world of fantasy, slumped against him and buried her face between his shoulder and chest.

"Hailey, sweet, look at me."

"No." She rolled her head against him in denial, because if she looked at him, she'd be lost. And with that one gesture, she knew she was admitting defeat. He *could*—he *had*—seduced her.

"Look at me. Please."

She raised her eyes, filled with tears of an emotion she couldn't name, and looked at him.

"Never tell me you aren't beautiful. Do you hear me?"

She could only nod dumbly, because he was still

touching her with more intimacy than any other human being ever had.

"Kiss me," he said.

With no hesitation, she lifted her mouth to his descending lips. With erotic symbolism, his tongue rubbed against hers as each of his fingers, in turn, touched her nipples.

"Oh, God," he grated, falling away from her. His breath was harsh and uneven. He stared at the decking beneath his feet for a long time before he looked up at her ruefully. With the gentleness one would use on a child, he raised the straps of her dress and rebuttoned the button he had undone.

"If I don't leave you now, I won't be able to keep my promise and go slowly." His hands came up once more to cup her face. "But God, you're delicious."

He kissed her with excruciating tenderness, slipping his tongue into her mouth only far enough to touch the tip of hers. "Good night, my love," he said. Then he was gone, disappearing into the rain.

Hailey let herself in and prepared for bed in a state of euphoria. He didn't intend to use her. He liked her for herself, not for what she could do for him, sexually or any other way. Had he only intended to use her, he wouldn't have left her tonight.

He had promised to seduce her, but it would be a seduction by design, exercising finesse and tenderness, perhaps even ... love? Love? She shivered with expectation at the thought. He had called her his love, but had the endearment meant anything? She knew from a lifetime of painful experience that people often paid lip service to love as a means of manipulation.

Tyler, the Tyler who had kissed her with such passionate care, wouldn't be that cruel.

CHAPTER 5

Guest Relations. Miss Ashton speaking," Hailey said into the telephone.

She had been at the park only half an hour, but her desk was already piled with mail and messages. There was a steady stream of guests entering the park turnstiles, though she had noticed earlier that the demographics of the crowd had changed in the past couple of weeks. Since school had started in most communities, the people who were visiting the park these days made an older, more sedate crowd.

"Good morning, Miss Ashton. Guess who this is."

She didn't have to guess. That voice had filled her dreams the entire restful night. Had she ever slept so well? She had awakened this morning still rosily aglow with remembrances of the past evening.

"Is this the man on the radio who gives away the prize money?"

"Nope."

"Darn. I don't have any luck. Are you the man who

is always calling me to ask if he can clean my uphol-
stery, drapes, and carpets for one low price?"

"Wrong again."

"I know you're not my breather, he—"

"What breather?" The voice on the other end
dropped its humor and became demandingly gruff.

Hailey laughed. "I was only seeing if you were paying attention."

"Good morning," he repeated. His tone changed
again. This time to a private pitch. He might well have
been speaking to her across a pillow.

"Good morning," she whispered back.

He cleared his throat "Things at the park okay? I
talked to Harmon earlier and he seemed to think so."

"Yes. Or as okay as things can be two weeks before
closing. A few guests are complaining that some of the
concession stands are closed. I've explained that many
of our employees are students and that, come September, they go back to school, making it necessary for us
to close some of the park's attractions. They grumble,
but they have to have something to complain about."

"You handle it all with aplomb."

"Thank you, sir."

"Will you miss me while I'm gone?"

Her heart plummeted and she gripped the receiver
with a hand grown suddenly lifeless. "Gone?" she
asked thinly.

"Yes, I'm afraid so. I've got to go to Atlanta for a
few days. I'm on the run now, but I wanted to call you

before I left. I have a plane to catch in Knoxville, and if I don't hurry, I'm not going to make it."

"I see." She felt like she had been dashed with cold water and then wrung out. Her spirit was deflating with each passing second. *You should have known, Hailey . . .*

"I'm leaving Faith here in the care of a lady the management of the Glenstone found for me. I think they'll get along fine, but the lady doesn't drive, and I wondered if you'd mind Faith's company on any outing you might be taking. I'd consider it a big favor."

Time seemed to stand still, as did her heart. She stared at the calendar on her desk until the demarcating lines between the days of the week bled together and her vision doubled.

"Hailey? Are you still there?"

"Yes." She spoke with amazing calm. Cool, dependable, competent Hailey. Nothing shook her. She could be counted on in any situation. "Yes, I'm still here."

Taking that as compliance with his request, he rushed on. "Thanks, Hailey. I didn't think you'd mind. The two of you get on so well. You're good for her."

Every word struck like a knife stabbing into her soul. She wanted to get on well with *Tyler.* She wanted to be good for *him.* He hadn't asked her how she had slept. He hadn't told her how difficult it had been for him to leave her last night. He had inquired about Serendipity and now he was asking her to be a glorified baby-sitter for his daughter. Damn the man!

"I might be busy, but I'll see what I can do. Is there anything else?" she asked with businesslike abruptness. "I'd hate for you to miss your plane, and I'm extremely busy myself."

"Hailey." She recognized the drugging quality in his voice now. It had obliterated her good sense on two occasions, but now she saw it for the sham that it was.

"I have another call, Mr. Scott. Good-bye." She slammed the receiver back onto the phone and then shouted at it, "And I hope you rot in hell."

The walls began closing in around her. If she didn't get out of that room, she would smother. She strode through the outer office. "I'm going to check something out, Charlene. Take my calls."

Then she was weaving her way through the park's landscaped walkways, not caring where she was going, knowing only that she must keep moving.

How could she have been so stupid not to have seen it? It had been there all the time, but she wasn't looking in that direction. When he first tried to woo her, she had thought he was availing himself of a willing playmate for the office. She should have known better than that. Someone with Tyler Scott's sterling reputation in the professional world hadn't gotten it by dallying with secretaries or associates.

What he *had* been looking for was a stand-in nanny for a daughter he was too busy and too selfish to care for himself. At her first sign of capitulation to his seduction scheme, he had taken a tentative step toward anchoring her in that position.

"Excuse me," Hailey mumbled as she swiftly passed a couple who were poring over a map of the park.

"Say, lady, you work here, don'tcha? Can you tell us where the Haunted Plantation House is? It's not on the map."

Of course it's on the map, you idiot! she wanted to scream. Instead, she answered with the patience and kindness of a nun. "Yes, sir. Here it is." She pointed to the plainly marked attraction on the colorful, easily read map. "Go past the puppet theater and you can't miss it."

"Okay," he said and ambled off with his wife in tow.

"You're welcome," Hailey muttered under her breath in exasperation. The rudeness of some people never ceased to amaze her. Which brought her immediately back to dark thoughts about the character of Tyler Scott.

Had he come to her like a decent human being, told her how much his daughter had taken to her, explained the girl's difficulties in adjusting emotionally to her mother's death, she would have sympathized. More than likely she would have *offered* to see Faith frequently. After all, she had very little that occupied her free time, and she enjoyed Faith.

But he hadn't made that approach.

He had appealed to her feminine vanity, to the instinctive need in every woman to feel attractive and . . . loved. He had plied her with compliments she should have seen through immediately. She had never been beautiful. Why had she been so eager to believe him when Tyler had told her she was? If her body was the sort that drove men wild with desire, wouldn't she have known about it before now? What a fool she had been.

The morning air was still crisp and cool, yet her cheeks burned as she recalled how she had shamelessly responded to his caresses, his honeyed words, his kisses. How he must have secretly gloated over his rapid conquest. He hadn't left her last night out of respect, as she had wanted to believe. He had left because he already had her malleable—like clay in his hands—ready to do his bidding, grant his favors.

To hell with your favors, Mr. Scott.

Since she had not paid attention to where she was going, her feet came to an abrupt standstill when she looked up and saw the Sidewinder. It was here, almost on this exact spot, that she had first met those gray eyes. They could compel her to behave in so uncharacteristic a way that she didn't even know herself anymore.

She imagined him the way she had first seen him, and she knew in that instant that the emotion rioting inside her was only half anger. The rest was bitter despair. She had grown to like him. Was dangerously close, she feared, to loving him. *Why, Tyler?* she asked the vision in her mind's eye. *Why couldn't you like me for myself? Why is it you only wanted to use me?*

Defeat and dejection rode heavily on her shoulders as she turned and walked back to her office. She didn't see that the trees were becoming tinted with the russets and golds of fall. She didn't realize how the autumn colors around her emphasized her own coloring.

Women turned envious eyes on her tall slender figure, her burnished hair, her green eyes, made luminous now by unshed tears. But Hailey didn't see their covert glances. Nor did she see how men turned to appreciate her proud carriage, the natural, unaffected sway of her hips, her well-shaped legs, her high breasts. She was blind to their approving looks and always had been. In her mirror she still saw herself as she had been in her youth—awkward, plain, undesirable.

She wasn't the only victim of Tyler's desertion. Faith called her that afternoon. "Daddy said I could call you if I had a problem, but he told me not to bother you too much. Am I bothering you?"

The loneliness in the soft voice tugged at Hailey's conscience. She couldn't take out her anger with the father on the child. "Of course not. *Do* you have a problem?"

"Well, sort of," Faith hedged, and Hailey got the distinct impression that she was stalling, searching for an excuse to have called. "Do you think I should perm my hair? You know, kinda like Stevie Nicks."

Hailey bit her lip to keep from laughing. "I think we should talk it over during dinner."

"You mean it, Hailey? Gee, that would be terrific." The whining had disappeared and exuberance had taken its place.

"Why don't we drive over to Pigeon Forge and eat there?"

"Okay! What should we wear?" Faith asked with a grown-up inflection, and Hailey wondered if she were imitating her late mother.

"We'll go sloppy in jeans and T-shirts. Let's go to a place where they have a huge salad bar and then we'll have two desserts."

Faith was giggling. "We'll both get fat and then when Daddy comes back, he won't know either of us."

Hailey thought that Tyler certainly wouldn't know her. She wouldn't be cooperative and eager the way she'd been the night before, telling him with actions, if not with words, how much she craved his touch, his kiss. "I'll pick you up at seven. I'm taking off early tonight." If she were going to be rebellious, she was going all the way. "Tell the manager—"

"Harry."

"Tell Harry I'll have you back by ten."

"Okay, see ya." Just before she hung up, Faith added, "Daddy said you'd think up neat things for us to do."

So, Hailey thought as she sat in her office tight-lipped and fuming, he had expected her to follow his wishes. He had foreseen no problems with her granting him this favor.

She had calmed down by the time she picked up Faith at the hotel. They had a fun evening, competing in a game of miniature golf after enjoying a huge country dinner. They spent each evening after that together.

Hailey enjoyed the girl, who was beginning to talk about some of the heartaches she had suffered. Hailey listened and knew instinctively that no one had given the child such undivided attention before. Once the floodgate had been let down, Faith's innermost anxieties spilled out.

The only fly in the ointment, for Hailey at least, was Faith's constant references to her father. To her, Tyler was a paragon of the male sex—physically, intellectually, morally. Hailey pretended for the girl's sake that she found him equally wonderful.

She had heard the word "Daddy" so often that when Faith shrieked it from across the indoor pool at Glenstone Lodge late one evening, Hailey didn't at first realize that he was actually there, standing before her, looking down at her as she lounged on one of the poolside chaises.

From the page of her novel, her eyes flew up to his with the same suicidal determination of a moth flying into a flame. For breathless seconds they stared at each other before he broke the eye contact to turn around and call to Faith. "Who is that graceful mermaid I see swimming out there?"

"Oh, Daddy," Faith said, blushing. Then she called, "Watch me. Watch now." With that she plunged beneath the surface and her two spindly legs pushed out of the water. They swayed like a pair of unsteady flagpoles as she did her handstand on the bottom of the pool.

When she was once again standing in the waist-deep water, beaming over her accomplishment, Tyler grinned broadly and applauded. "You've been practicing." While Faith was swimming to the side of the pool, he turned back to Hailey. "How long have you been lying here, in that indecent swimsuit, providing the ogling yokels the kind of visions that dreams are made of?"

She didn't want him to tease her with clever words, she didn't want him to look thoroughly masculine, and sexy enough to turn the head of every woman who chanced to pass by. When he looked at her the way he did now and spoke with that soft, low, seductive purr, she couldn't think. Her memory blurred and she had a hard time remembering why she despised him so.

Before she once again made a monumental fool of herself, she sat up, swung her legs over the edge of the chair and asked, "Did you have a nice trip?"

"Boring business meetings," he said, tugging on Faith's pigtails as she ran up to him. Playfully, he shook the water he squeezed out of them off his hands.

Hailey dumped her book into her large shoulder bag and stood up, pulling on her terry-cloth wrapper.

"Where are you going, Hailey?" Faith asked. Her chin was dripping water onto her bony chest. Her skin and lips were turning slightly blue as she shivered. Her eyes looked myopic without her glasses.

"I'd better go on home."

"But we were—"

"What were your plans?" Tyler addressed the question to Faith rather than to Hailey.

"Hailey brought her clothes over and after we swam, we were going out to dinner."

"Sounds good to me," Tyler said heartily. "Can you wait for me to take a quick dip, too?"

"Sure!" Faith said. Then she looked hesitantly at Hailey. "Can't we, Hailey?"

If Hailey refused either to wait for him or go to dinner, she would have to make explanations to Faith. At that moment she didn't feel up to doing more than nodding her head in agreement "Sure, that's fine."

Tyler's eyes were probing hers, but he looked away to chuck Faith under the chin before he said, "I'll be right back."

In minutes he had returned, entering the atrium by a side door and walking toward the pool with all the confidence and nonchalance of a pagan god. And almost as nakedly.

His swimming trunks were black with white piping around his trim legs. They hugged his hips with a fit that made Hailey want to stare when she knew propriety dictated she should glance away quickly. The muscles of his thighs were lean but hinted at tremendous strength beneath his hair-roughened skin.

Hailey tried to avert her eyes from his torso, but was powerless to do so. He had the physique of a man half his age; his maturity only heightened his virility. His shoulders and chest were muscular, but not bulky. His ribs and waist were trim, but not thin. He looked powerful, but was graceful as he executed a knife-blade dive that barely made a ripple on the surface of the water.

Hailey had gone to sit in the whirlpool at one corner of the poolroom. The atrium ceiling was three stories above her, yet the indoor pool with its grotto design, complete with waterfall and lavalike rocks, had an aura of intimacy about it. The tropical plants around the pool grew in profusion in the steamy atmosphere.

Tyler and Faith were playing and splashing boisterously in the larger pool. Hailey lay back in the hot, bubbly water and closed her eyes. Projected on the back of her lids was an image of Tyler. She knew what it was like to touch that dark, springy hair that grew at the top of his chest. But what of that narrow, silky line that grew straight as an arrow down his stomach and disappeared into the waistband of his trunks? What was it like to touch that?

"I'd like to be inside your head and see what naughty thought has brought such a sublime expression to your face."

Her eyes sprang open, and she was disconcerted to see that he was in the whirlpool with her. The churning water had kept her from hearing him as he stepped in. He sat down beside her on the underwater bench and whispered, "In fact, I'd like to be inside you—period."

She struggled to sit up straight and was almost unbalanced by the force of the swirling water. "Don't talk to me like that!" she hissed.

He smiled lazily. "Why?"

"*Why!* Because we're in a public place, that's why."

"We have the place to ourselves."

She looked around in desperation and saw that he was right. Where had everyone gone? "Your daughter is here."

"She's playing under the waterfall. She can't hear us."

"Still, you . . . Oh! What is that?"

"My hand."

His boldness shocked her. "Tyler . . ." His name was spoken like a verbal caress and not the reprimand she had intended. Frantically she groped for the hand that wouldn't be captured or deterred. Where was all that cool condescension she was going to treat him to? That well-planned contempt? The disparaging glances? Within minutes of his return he had her once again at his mercy—confused, breathless.

"Tyler, please. You shouldn't."

"Why?" he asked against the corner of her mouth.

"Because . . . because . . ." She searched her mind for a plausible reason but could find none. It felt so good to have his hand squeezing the tender flesh on the inside of her thigh. His fingers moved without discretion or shame, gliding over her skin as sleekly as did the soothing water. Her eyes closed and her head fell back against her shoulders. Unwilling to admit total surrender, she still denied his right to take such liberties. "Because you shouldn't," she argued lamely.

"You can touch any part of me you want to."

That intriguing line of hair that ran from his chest to abdomen came unbidden to her mind. Her eyelids fluttered open to see him staring down into her face. One thick brow was raised in an amused query, while his lips twitched with controlled laughter. "Do you already have some part in mind?"

She struggled against him. His insolence infuriated her, and all the pent-up anger that had been simmering inside her boiled to the surface with volcanic force. "Let me go." Extricating herself from his persistent hands, she managed to stand and walk up the shallow steps of the pool. "From now on, keep your hands to yourself," she said with venom.

She waved to Faith from the side of the pool. "Come on out so we can dress for dinner." When the girl climbed out of the water, Hailey wrapped a towel around her and together they walked to Tyler's suite of rooms. A sitting room divided the two bedrooms, and the smaller of them had been given over for Faith's use.

Faith had claimed the shower first, so Hailey was rinsing out their suits in the basin when she heard a knock on the connecting door. Cursing softly under her breath, she slipped her terry wrapper over her nakedness and went to the door. "Yes?"

"I came to borrow some soap."

"Soap."

"Yeah, you know that stuff that bubbles and foams in the water."

She ignored his attempted humor. "Where is yours?"

"If I knew, would I be borrowing more?"

She stepped into the bathroom where Faith's off-key rendition of a popular rock song could be heard over the shower's spray. She picked up an unwrapped bar of hotel soap and opened the door a crack to offer it to him.

He moved with lightning speed. Her wrist was grasped in an iron grip and she was hauled through the door and tossed unceremoniously onto the sofa of the sitting room. He lay atop her, pinning her to the yielding cushions. Her robe fell open. His hard thighs moved against hers. Her arms were held on either side of her head by strong fingers locked around her wrists. Their breathing was loud and rapid in the still room where Faith's singing was only a dim echo.

"Let's have it," he demanded.

"Let me up."

"Not a chance. Not until I know what burr has gotten under your saddle."

"I don't know what you mean."

"Like hell you don't. I knew something was wrong when I called you before I left for Atlanta, but I didn't have time to pursue it then. Now I'm back and you're as prickly as a porcupine again, shooting daggers every time those green eyes light on me. I want to know why."

"Nothing's the matter," she declared vehemently and renewed her efforts at release. His hold only became more tenacious.

"Then you'll be wanting to kiss me as much as I've been wanting to kiss you."

His lips came down on hers hard and insistent. She resisted, clenching her jaws together, refusing to respond to the hateful desire that even now was winding through her body.

He lifted his head and stared down into her stormy eyes. "Okay, my stubborn lady. You want to be persuaded. I won't disappoint you."

He lowered his head and nibbled at the skin on the side of her neck. His hair was a silky caress itself as he moved his head lower to rest against her chest. He kissed his way to the underside of her arm. "I missed you. Obstinate as you are, I missed you like hell."

She sucked in her breath sharply as his lips opened over her skin. How is it she had never heard of that erogenous zone? His tongue skimmed it, touching it with fire, and a moan issued out of her throat. Futilely, she struggled to lower her arm and end this torment, but he refused to allow it. "You like that? We've only just started, Hailey."

She fought the sinking feeling in the pit of her stomach, fought the liquid heaviness that throbbed between her thighs. Her mind screamed that she hated him, but the only sound that formed in her heart and on her lips was his name, catechistically repeated.

"Yes, my love. Look at how beautiful you are." His eyes swept her length. "All week I fantasized about seeing you naked beneath me. I wanted to see these breasts that I had only touched in the dark. You're more beautiful than I ever anticipated."

His mouth sampled the side of her breast and she

writhed against him. One of his knees insinuated its way between her thighs. It was an invasion that met no resistance. His swimming trunks were still damp as his hips settled in a complementing position over hers. Behind that scant piece of cloth, she felt his desire.

"So sweet," he whispered. His tongue painted a swathe of white heat on the undercurve of her breasts. She could feel his eyes touching her before his breath fanned the nipples that seemed to beg for his touch.

So lightly that she might have imagined it, his lips brushed one pink bud. But she didn't imagine the second light touch of his mouth, nor the damp flicking of his tongue. "Tyler," she said urgently as his mouth closed around her.

Her hands were freed, but they sought bondage of another kind in the thick mass of his hair. Her fingers plowed through it, holding his head against her, silently beseeching him never to cease that gentle tugging that transmitted tiny pinpricks of feeling to the center of her being.

Her other breast was blessed with the same ardent attention. He spoke love words against her warm, scented skin even as he rained kisses on it.

When at last he raised himself above her and peered into her eyes, now slumberous with passion, he asked, "Will you kiss me now?"

"Yes." Consent sounded like supplication. "Yes, Tyler. Kiss me."

His mouth fused with hers. They allowed themselves no unnecessary movement, savoring the taste, the feel, the essence of the other while they drank thirstily. When at long last they indulged themselves in play, their tongues battled in a sexual skirmish.

It was while his tongue was exploring the fragile skin behind her ear that he murmured, "Now, aren't you sorry you wasted all that precious time on hostility?"

If he had slapped her, she couldn't have been brought up more sharply. What had happened? When had she lost control? My God! she thought. Had she forgotten the reason behind all his fervent pseudo-lovemaking? Her resolve had been to scorn the man, to spurn his romantic tricks. Instead, she was lying naked beneath him, begging him with every fiber of her being to take her, to use her.

She put the heels of her hands against his shoulders and shoved with all her might. Taking him completely off-guard, she sent him rolling off her and onto his back on the floor. She bolted to her feet, yanking the terry cloth closed over her feverish body. "Is this the way you pay all your baby-sitters?"

CHAPTER 6

Just before she whirled toward the door, she had the pleasure of seeing him completely dumbfounded. He sat staring up at her with blinking, uncomprehending eyes. She reached the door connecting the two rooms just as Faith turned off the taps in the shower. She closed the door behind her with emphasis.

Quickly she gathered her things together. She wasn't about to spend the evening in the company of that man, even at the risk of hurting Faith's feelings.

Faith stepped out of the bathroom clad only in her underwear. "Hailey, are you ready to French-braid my hair? You said we should do it before it dried too much."

Inwardly Hailey groaned, but she answered brightly. "Of course I'm ready."

She settled Faith on the bed and combed through the straight, wet strands. Sectioning it off, she began to weave the hair into two French braids that started close to Faith's hairline and ended at two ribboned pigtails at her shoulders.

"Gee, it looks so neat. I wish I could learn to do it."

"It's almost impossible to do on oneself. I learned by doing Ellen's hair."

While still admiring her new hairdo in the mirror over the dresser, Faith said, "You'd better hurry and get ready. I don't think Daddy likes having to wait."

Hailey took Faith's shoulders gently under her hands and turned the girl toward her. "Faith, would you be too terribly disappointed if I begged off tonight? I'm very tired and I need an evening at home to catch up on my laundry—things like that. You understand, don't you?" When she could see that Faith didn't understand and was about to object to the change in plans, she rushed on. "Besides, it's been almost a week since your daddy has seen you. I think he'd enjoy an evening spent exclusively with you."

Faith cast a quick glance toward the connecting door. "You really think so?"

"Yes. The two of you probably have a lot to talk about since you haven't seen each other for several days."

"I don't know." Faith didn't sound at all convinced. "He likes talking to you, too. You're closer to his age."

If Hailey hadn't been so shattered by what had happened just minutes before, she could have laughed at Faith's naive observation. "I still think it would be better if I left now."

Putting action to words, she got into her clothes. Picking up the dress she had planned on wearing to dinner and the oversized handbag she had taken to the pool, she went to the door. "Your father already knows I'm not coming with you." It was a blatant lie, but if Tyler could use deceptive tactics, so could she. She knew he wouldn't reveal her lie to Faith. "I'll call you tomorrow, okay?"

"Okay," Faith mumbled dispiritedly. Then she brightened and looked at Hailey hopefully. "Do you think Daddy will like my hair this way?" Her appeal was so pitiable that Hailey leaned down and kissed her lightly on the cheek.

"He'll think you're stunning. Have a good time, and I'll talk to you tomorrow."

Hailey didn't breathe deeply until she was halfway home. Any second she expected to see the Lincoln looming up in her rearview mirror, but apparently she had made good her escape. On the other hand, Tyler probably didn't care if she went to dinner with them tonight or not. His romantic advances had been thwarted, and a man as virile as he certainly wouldn't waste his time and trouble on anyone who put up a fight. He'd find a more cooperative woman.

Her hands were shaking as she let herself through the front door. Why should the thought of Tyler with another woman cloak her with a stifling depression? The idea of his kissing someone else with the same passion, touching someone else with the same familiarity as he had kissed and touched her, filled her with desperation.

Deciding to work it off and to salve her conscience for lying to Faith, she did her laundry, her hair, her nails, and paid bills. Stacking the sealed, stamped envelopes on the table near the door where she would see them in the morning and put them in the mailbox, she decided she might just as well go to bed. Her chores hadn't rid her of her earlier depression.

Indeed they had only pointed out the tedium of her life. She found herself wondering where Tyler and Faith had eaten. Surely their dinner had been more exciting than her bowl of canned soup. What had Tyler said and done when he learned she had run out? Had he been irritated? Had he cared?

She was switching out the lamp on her bedside table when the telephone rang. Her heart jumped, skidded, then began beating wildly. Would it be—could it be—Tyler? Did she want to hear his voice? Denying that she did, she prayed that she would as she picked up the receiver.

"Hailey? Harmon here."

She sagged with disappointment. "Hello, Harmon."

"Sorry if I woke you up, but I just heard from the head honcho. He's back from wherever he went and is on a rampage. He's called a department heads' meeting for eight o'clock tomorrow morning. Set your alarm an hour early. I'm advising everyone not to be late. I don't think he's in a forgiving mood."

She swallowed. "D . . . do you know what got him upset?"

"Upset is putting it mildly. I only hope it wasn't something I did that got him so bent out of shape. See you in the morning."

He hung up, and for a long moment Hailey didn't even realize he had. Worriedly, she gnawed her bottom lip. Unlike the general manager of Serendipity, she *knew* what had made Tyler Scott angry. She only hoped none of her colleagues would find out.

It was a tense group that sat around the long, wide conference table in the room adjacent to Harmon's office. Anxiety hung over them like a pall. Nancy had made coffee, but few were availing themselves of it. They were all executive-level employees, but they were nervous. It was unnerving that an employer who had remained a mystery for years had suddenly become actively involved in Serendipity's daily operations. Didn't he trust them to run the park anymore? Who had made a mistake? Was Tyler Scott going to fire them all this morning?

Tyler swept through the door and went directly to the head of the table, where no one had had the temerity to sit. Hailey kept her gaze on the American flag standing in the corner of the room, though out of the corner of her eye, she saw Tyler's clothing and was surprised. She had expected a business suit. Instead he had on a pair of jeans and a sport shirt. The soft yellow color contrasted with his darkly tanned features and the shirt revealed the hard muscles that she was coming to know all too well. She swallowed around the lump in her throat and kept her eyes resolutely on the flag.

"Good morning," he said with the enthusiasm of a

judge saying, "You've been found guilty." He was answered by a chorus of cautious replies.

"We have a problem," he said as he slapped a thick folder of papers on the polished surface of the table. No one moved. "Serendipity is making me too much money."

Twelve pairs of eyes swept the length of the table. Disbelief was registered on each face. When each had confirmed that he hadn't heard incorrectly, all heads turned back to the man at the head of the table. He was smiling. The nervous laughter of relief rippled through the room.

"Thanks to all of you, Serendipity has done well this past season. I've made a hefty profit, which the IRS is ready to pounce on unless I turn it back into the company. I'm looking for ways to spend money," he said, tossing the pencil he had been playing with onto the table and leaning back in his chair. "Get creative."

"Do you mean ways to spend it in addition to the new rides we discussed, Mr. Scott?" the Director of Operations asked him timidly.

"You're off the hook, Davis," Tyler said, smiling. "For the benefit of you others I'll announce the purchase of three new rides from a German company. They'll be installed and ready to go by the opening of our next season. Davis and I have already taken care of that. Harrison," he turned toward the Director of Grounds Maintenance, "we expect the rides to be delivered in January. As soon as they're set up, you'll landscape them. Check out the sites now, go over the plans for their layout, then start charting your land-scaping. Order whatever you want. Be extravagant."

"Yes, sir."

"And in the meantime, embellish existing landscap-ing wherever you see fit."

"Yes, sir."

"Okay, let's hear from some of you others."

The Director of Personnel, whose sense of humor was well known, said, "We could all stand a raise."

Everyone laughed, including Tyler. "You've got it. Fifteen percent, retroactive from the first of the sea-son." The audible gasp around the table was followed by spontaneous applause. Tyler managed to look hum-ble. To the Director of Personnel, he said, "And raise the minimum wage, too. We want only the most able kids running our park. I'm willing to pay more to get them. Screen them carefully when you begin hiring next year."

"Yes, sir."

To Hailey's vast relief, Tyler had studiously ignored her since opening the discussion. Now she came under the piercing scrutiny of his gray eyes. "We haven't heard from you, Miss Ashton. Any ideas?"

She wasn't about to cower under his incisive tone. She was ready for him. "Yes, Mr. Scott. I do have an idea." He indicated with a wave of his hand that she was to continue. "From all the surveys my department takes, from every questionnaire it gets back, the main complaint concerns the long waiting lines for the most popular attractions."

"We can't help the waiting lines. It stands to reason that the better the attraction, the longer the line."

"No, we can't eliminate the lines, but we could alleviate the boredom." She had everyone's attention. "I suggest having a live band—country perhaps, or Dixieland—which would go from ride to ride entertaining the people standing in line. I'm talking about ten or twelve costumed musicians who could ride on a small wagon or even walk through the park. I've also thought that a clever magician could work the crowds, or maybe a fortune-teller. Someone who could easily banter with the public and hold their attention away from their long wait for the ride."

"Where does one find such traveling troubadours these days?" Tyler asked. He propped his elbows on the table as he leveled his eyes on her. Was he thinking about her desertion last night?

"You have a live show department. I would think the band, magician, etc., would fall under its auspices."

The director of that department shifted uncomfortably in his chair as all eyes in the room, including Tyler's, swung to him. "What about it, Newell? Do you think you can get such acts together?"

"Yes, sir. I think it's a good idea."

"Consult with Miss Ashton before doing anything. I want her to be involved on the project."

And so it went for the next half hour. Every department—Wardrobe, General Maintenance, Advertising and Public Relations, Food and Beverage, Gifts and

Souvenirs—was pressured for ways to improve, enlarge, and enhance.

Just before concluding the meeting, Tyler said, "Let's go out with a bang. As you can see, I'm here to work." He indicated his casual clothes. "I intend to go over every inch of the park before we close for the season. This last week of operation will be busy, especially this weekend. I want each of Serendipity's guests to have a good time. Thank you for a successful season."

Hailey was hoping to slip out of the conference room without attracting notice, but she was halted at the door. "Miss Ashton, I'd like to see you for a moment. Excuse me," Tyler said, shouldering through the others on their way out. He clasped the upper part of her arm and ushered her through the door. "I'll walk with you to the Guest Relations Office and we can talk on the way," he said for the benefit of the others.

It was a half hour before opening and the only foot traffic on the paved walkways was an occasional employee scurrying to his post. The pavement was still wet from the overnight washing it had gotten from the maintenance men. The glory of the summer flowers in the well-tended beds was waning, but the chrysanthemums were brilliant in their shades of copper and gold.

Hailey was stonily silent as she marched at Tyler's side, matching his long stride. She didn't want to think about how well his tight-fitting jeans suited the hard length of his legs. Or how the morning breeze, a brisk harbinger of fall, ruffled the dark hair falling on his forehead.

"I want to check this out," he said, taking her arm once again and leading her to the entrance of one of the attractions. It was an observation tower built to resemble a frontier stockade. It captured the flavor of historic Tennessee, but was thoroughly modernized, complete with an elevator.

"I have to get to work," Hailey objected, pulling uselessly on her arm.

"You *are* at work," Tyler growled. "Good morning," he said to the young man operating the elevator, effectively cutting off Hailey's chance to argue with him. The young man was dressed in a costume made to look like the fringed buckskins of a frontiersman.

"Good morning, Miss Ashton," he said deferentially, recognizing her at once. He nodded politely to Tyler.

"Good morning, Randy," she said, quickly reading his name tag.

"We'd like to go up on the platform, Randy," Tyler said.

The young man cast a permission-seeking glance at Hailey. "It's all right, Randy. This is Mr. Tyler Scott. He owns Serendipity."

The boy's face flooded with hot color. "Oh, yeah, sure. I . . . Sure," he stammered. "It's just you know, we're not supposed to let anyone . . . I mean . . ."

"You did just fine," Tyler assured him. "Now, may we go up? And please don't let anyone else go up until we come down. We're planning some innovations for next season."

"Sure thing, Mr. Scott."

Hailey knew she had been taken advantage of, but there wasn't anything she could do about it without embarrassing herself, not to mention poor Randy. Docilely she preceded Tyler into the elevator.

"Any aversion to heights?" he asked as the elevator whisked them up.

"The only aversion I have is to overbearing men."

"Then you couldn't possibly be referring to me because I'm the epitome of charm." He flashed her a devastating grin just as the doors to the elevator swished open. "Ladies first," he said mockingly, bowing from the waist.

She stamped out ahead of him, only to be caught before she had taken more than three steps and pulled around to face him. "Okay, Hailey. This has gone far enough. What did you mean by that enigmatic question about baby-sitters last night before you so cowardly sneaked out?"

"I didn't *sneak*," she countered hotly. "And I'm not a coward."

"No? I think using a child to wiggle out of a situation is cowardly."

"Don't talk to me about using people, Mr. Scott. I could take lessons from you."

"What the hell is that supposed to mean?"

"As if you didn't know. Using compliments and kisses to get yourself a free baby-sitter." There. She had said it. She raised her chin in triumph. Her victory was sweet and extremely short-lived. Tyler threw his head back and roared with laughter.

When it finally subsided, he looked down at her and said in a voice still rumbling with humor, "You have a very low opinion of yourself. A free baby-sitter? Is that what you thought I wanted you for?"

"Didn't you?" she asked haughtily.

He shook his head and tightened his fingers around her shoulders. "No, Hailey. Why would I be concerned about paying a baby-sitter?"

"It's not the money. It's that Faith likes me. Your conscience doesn't trouble you when you have to leave her, because you believe that I'll be a substitute for you."

"It's true that I'm glad you two get along so well. I told you that you're good for her and I meant it. If she despised you or vice versa, it would be harder for our relationship to flourish."

"Our . . . ? We have no relationship. We won't have one."

"Why do you fight it, Hailey?" He shook his head affectionately. "At the risk of infuriating you further, I'll tell you that I asked Harmon about you. Not in a way that would arouse his curiosity," he hastened to add when he felt her back stiffening. "I wanted to know about the other men in your life. He told me there had been no small number of men in park-related jobs who had tried to thaw the cold hauteur of Miss Ashton, but as far as he knew, none had succeeded.

Even Harmon, married as he is, got a wistful look on his face when he spoke of you."

"Don't be ridiculous."

"You see? That's what I'm talking about. Why is it ridiculous?"

"Because men don't think of me that way. I'm not the type."

He smiled tenderly. "Oh, you're the type all right. Why can't you believe that I want you for the woman you are without attaching some lurid motivation to it? First it was sexual harassment that might cost you your job. Now it's using you to provide a companion for my daughter. What outrageous accusations, Hailey."

He wrapped his arms around her and moved close, pressing her between the solid wall and his unyielding body. "The only thing I want to use you for is to slake this desire I have for you. And I want you to use me in the same way."

For a second, she was caught up in the seductive power of his gray eyes. She wanted to believe him. The loneliness she had suffered last night had been almost too much to bear. While he'd been away, she had missed him. Even though they had battled every time they saw each other, she had missed not seeing him, not hearing his voice. She wanted him in her life, yet . . . She straightened and said firmly, "I'm still your employee."

"Yes, you are. And you have the most beautiful breasts of anyone on the payroll."

"What—"

"I was looking at them just this morning down the length of that conference table while someone was rattling on about something—the wardrobe department, I think. Anyway, I was thinking about how they look when we're—"

"Tyler—"

"Kissing. They're beautifully shaped. Full and round—"

"Tyler!"

"White and dusky—"

"Please," she groaned.

"I'm going to keep talking like this until you kiss me. And when I touch them—"

She went up on tiptoe and pressed his lips with hers. He opened his mouth, sent his tongue on an erotic venture between her lips, and pulled her inexorably closer to his hard frame. He kissed her with a passion that, in his opinion, had been cruelly left unsatisfied the day before.

Hailey didn't combat the need within her to kiss him back. She strained against him in a way that would have shocked her only weeks ago. Under the soothing strokes of his hands between her blazer and her blouse, she moved invitingly.

"We'll continue this discussion after dinner at your house tonight," Tyler said between the kisses he was showering on her mouth. "I'll bring the steaks and wine. You provide everything else. Eight o'clock?"

"Yes," she sighed, unable at that point to refuse him anything.

Trancelike, she rode down with him in the elevator. He tucked a telltale curl behind her ear seconds before the doors came open. Randy was waiting for them anxiously. "Everything okay up there?"

"Everything was perfect," Tyler said, slanting a knowing glance at Hailey.

"Thanks," Randy said as they walked away from him.

"I'm on my way to Sanders's office, Miss Ashton, if you should need me," Tyler said loud enough for Randy to hear.

"Thank you, Mr. Scott."

He turned away, only to stop, snap his fingers, and call back to her. "Oh, Miss Ashton?"

"Yes?"

He came up to her, put his mouth directly next to her ear and whispered, "I meant what I said about your breasts."

She found herself studying that part of her anatomy as she stepped out of the shower late that evening. Looking at her reflection in the full-length mirror on the back of her bathroom door, she decided that her shape wasn't too bad for a woman her age. Her slimness, which she had cursed in adolescence, she now looked on as a blessing. Her slender figure took years off her age.

All day she had been in a state of anticipation, looking forward to her dinner with Tyler. He hadn't quite convinced her that his motives for wanting to seduce her had nothing to do with either her work or his daughter. She smiled as she slipped into her underwear. Was it possible she was looking forward to more of his convincing?

Whether she was or not, she certainly had chosen a seductive outfit for their dinner, she thought as she stepped into black silk pants and pulled on an open-weave knit top. She knew she wore black well. It contrasted with her vibrant hair and fair complexion. Tonight she decided to forget her usual inhibitions and see what happened. She let her hair dry naturally and put large gold loops in her ears. Her fragrance was subtle but undeniably there. Beneath the revealing knit top, she wore a black, lace-trimmed camisole.

Not bad, she thought, eyeing herself critically in the mirror one more time. Certainly a departure from the prim and proper, competent, no-nonsense Miss Ashton.

But what would Tyler think of her? As she went through the house, checking last-minute details, she wondered at her rapid heartbeat and the catch in her throat each time she thought of the night to come. She hadn't had all that much experience with men. *Could* she trust him to mean what he said? Did he find her beautiful? Desirable? Sexy?

The salad of three varieties of lettuce, black olives, cherry tomatoes, and artichoke hearts was chilling in the refrigerator. The foil-wrapped potatoes were baking in the oven while their trimmings of sour cream, chives, and bacon bits had already been arranged on a tray. Chocolate mousse was firming in parfait glasses.

Everything was ready. Except for Hailey. She was a jumble of nerves. So much so that she jumped when she heard his car door slam and his quick tread on the decking.

Taking three deep breaths, and hoping that her hair wouldn't riot out of control too soon, she went to let him in. The look on his face when she opened the door should have dispelled her qualms. His jaw dropped open and his eyes traveled her length several times before coming to rest on her face. He didn't speak until each feature had been properly admired.

"You look ravishing. Come to think of it, that's a terrific idea. Let's skip dinner and I'll ravish you right now."

She laughed nervously and placed a hand at the base of her throat to still the palpitation there. "You're dripping something."

He looked down at the pan he was carrying in one hand. "Oops, sorry." He pushed past her and went through the louvered doors into the kitchen. "I've had the chef at the hotel marinating these steaks for me all day." He set the aluminum pan with its foil covering on the countertop and turned to her.

"Faith?" she asked softly.

"Isn't coming. Tonight is strictly rated 'adults only.' "

"Oh." She was ashamed of feeling so glad that they would be alone.

His brows lowered over his sultry eyes. "Come here." His voice was gentle—soft, but commanding.

As one hypnotized, Hailey walked to him. His hands stroked up the bare expanse of her arms, slipped under the sleeves of her top, and massaged her shoulders. "I like your hair that way," he said.

"Give it about an hour. It'll start going nineteen different directions. It's wild."

"I like savagery," he teased. "I'm feeling dangerously primitive myself right now." His voice was husky as he drew her closer. His hands moved to her back. Gifted fingers kneaded her spine. With the slightest pressure to the small of her back, he pulled her to him by slow degrees until their bodies met. She gasped as his virility seared like a brand through their clothes.

"See what you do to me?" He tilted his head downward and took her mouth under his.

Her mouth was a warm dark cave that his tongue explored with sensual leisure. It stroked the roof of her mouth, her teeth, the inside of her lips, until her breath was coming in short, light gasps. He was merciless, relentless. His hands slid under her hips, cradling them in his palms and bringing her against him.

A throbbing ache began to build deep inside her and she moved with him, knowing instinctively that he could relieve this wonderful ailment. Fitting herself more surely against him, she was awed at how perfectly the softness of her body cushioned the hardness of his.

•

He emitted a harsh cry as he tore his mouth from hers and buried his face in the hollow of her neck. His breathing was sporadic. "Hailey," he said in a low groan. "If you keep that up we might just as well forget the steaks and the wine and whatever you've prepared." His tongue flirted with the gold loop in her ear before his teeth captured her earlobe. His hands moved up from her waist and around her ribs to coast lightly over the sides of her breasts. "What do you say?"

It was hard to say anything. His mouth was working its magic on her ear. Her body was hot where it touched his. "I think," she started in a gruff voice, then cleared her throat, and continued. "I think that we should behave in a civilized manner and have our dinner as planned."

He sighed. Pulling away from her, he kissed her quickly on the mouth. "You're right. Can you cook as well as you can kiss?"

She laughed and looked at him coyly. "I've never had anyone compare the skills."

He swatted her bottom and said, "Well if your culinary talents come anywhere close to your . . . ah . . . other accomplishments, I'm in for a feast. I hope you didn't bother preparing a dessert. I already know what I'm having." His eyes toured her rapaciously.

"I left the wine in the car in an ice bucket. I'll go get it while you turn on the broiler."

He left her and for a moment she stood disoriented and trembling. When she tried to move, her legs felt wobbly—a side effect of the weakness his hands and mouth induced each time he touched her. She could feel the silly grin on her face, feel the joy bubbling inside her chest, feel the happiness welling up in her until it came out as a tuneless humming song while she lifted the juicy, dripping steaks onto the grill.

Tyler was feeling just as happy, she noted when she heard him laughing as he came through the front door. So hearty was his laugh that her curiosity was piqued, and she peered over the barroom door.

Her grin disappeared. Her bubble of happiness burst painfully. The song died on her lips.

The red-haired woman clinging to Tyler's arm let her eyes dance around the room until she sighted Hailey. "Hello, big sister," she called gaily.

"Hello, Ellen."

CHAPTER | 7

Why in the world would you let a gorgeous hunk like this out of your sight for one second, Hailey? Even if he was fetching a bottle of very expensive and very good wine." Ellen snuggled closer to Tyler and looked up at him beguilingly from under a veil of long, luxurious lashes.

"Maybe she doesn't think I'm a gorgeous hunk," Tyler said dryly. Hailey noted that he wasn't averse to the way Ellen was clinging to him or to the generous breast that rubbed against his arm.

Ellen's laugh was as light and musical as a tinkling bell. "Then I'd consider her demented." Ellen detached herself, trailing her well-manicured nails down Tyler's arm, and came toward Hailey. "Why are you hiding behind that door, Hailey? Haven't you got a hug for your baby sister?"

Hailey pushed through the swinging doors and met her sister halfway. She avoided Tyler's eyes as she accepted Ellen's enthusiastic embrace. He would be looking at Ellen with that assessing, hungry look with which all men looked at her. Hailey didn't think she could take that.

Tonight she had worked at looking sexy. To Ellen it came naturally. Her tight designer jeans and western-cut shirt, left unbuttoned to the middle of her chest, made a mockery of Hailey's slinky black ensemble. While Hailey had let her hair go natural, Ellen had chosen tonight to pull hers back into a sleek, sophisticated knot that only made Hailey look disheveled. She felt like a candle whose flame had been snuffed out.

"I'm glad to see you, Ellen," she lied. "I didn't expect you."

"That's obvious," Ellen drawled suggestively, and turned her head to wink at Tyler. "And I promise not to stay more than a moment. I drove from Nashville on an impulse to see you and I have to go right back."

"That's a long trip. What about your job?" Hailey asked worriedly.

"I called in sick after lunch. That's why I have to drive back tonight. I have to go in early in the morning to make up those hours."

Tyler had come up to Hailey and placed an arm around her shoulders. Hastily she said, "I'm sorry. Did you two introduce yourselves?"

"No. I'm Tyler Scott, Miss Ashton."

"Ellen," she said, laughing and shaking his extended hand. "I hope I'll be seeing you again."

Tyler glanced down at Hailey, but her head was bowed. She didn't see the warm look in his eyes. All she heard was his response, which was a promise. "You will."

"Hailey," Ellen said tentatively, "I really need to be getting on my way again. Could we—"

"I'll see to the steaks," Tyler said, taking Ellen's hint. He squeezed Hailey's shoulder before releasing it and going into the kitchen.

"Let's go in your bedroom," Ellen said in a stage whisper and grabbed Hailey's hand, pulling her along after her.

She closed the door behind them and leaned against it, her eyes wide. "My God, Hailey, where have you been hiding him? How long has this been going on? Who is he? Where did you meet him? Tell me all."

Hailey crossed the room to her dresser and automatically picked up her hairbrush. She began tearing it through her tumble of coppery curls. "There's really not much to tell. I've only known him a few weeks. I actually met him through his daughter, who was stung by a bee on their outing to Serendipity."

"He's loaded. That car! And those designer clothes."

Some perverse need to shock her sister made Hailey say offhandedly, "He owns Serendipity. That and a lot of other things."

"Jeez, sis, when you score, you score big. I'll bet he's dynamite in bed." The hairbrush remained poised over Hailey's head for a frozen instant, but then came down to punish the tangled strands again. "Well?" Ellen demanded impatiently.

"Well, what?"

"How is he in bed?"

Hailey caught Ellen's reflection in the mirror. Her eyes were gleaming with imagination run rampant. Again, Hailey wanted to flaunt the fact that a man like Tyler was spending the evening alone with her. "Just as you guessed," she heard herself say. "He's dynamite." The hairbrush slipped from her fingers and clattered to the dresser top as if underlining her lie. Why did she want to let Ellen go on thinking she and Tyler had slept together? She twisted her hair into a tight knot and gouged her scalp as she viciously secured it with pins.

"Oh, sis, I'm glad you're so happy." Ellen's sigh was theatrical and transparent. Hailey decided to wait her out. This time she wasn't going to ask what was wrong. "I'm glad *one* of us is happy."

With an inward sigh, Hailey took the bait. "You aren't? I thought you liked your new job and new friends."

"Friends! Huh! You know the girl I was telling you about, the one who was being so nice to me?" Ellen didn't wait for an answer. "Well, she's turned out to be a real bitch. I owe her a little money, which she practically *forced* me to borrow from her, and now she wants it all back at once. Honestly, don't people trust each other anymore?"

Hailey turned around to face Ellen, who was now sitting Indian-fashion in the middle of the bed, looking younger than Faith. Tears were shining in her green eyes. "How much is a 'little'?" Hailey asked unsym-pathetically.

"Five hundred dollars," was the mumbled reply.

"What!" Hailey gasped, truly shocked. "Ellen, how could you? Five hundred dollars? For what?"

"Don't shout at me, Hailey," Ellen sobbed. "I told you she practically forced me to borrow it."

"I don't believe you."

"She did! You're being just as mean to me as she is."

"Where did the money go?" Sickening thoughts of drugs, gambling, and extortion raced through Hailey's mind. "What did you spend it on?"

"Clothes mostly. Some jewelry. Don't look at me like that, Hailey," Ellen cried, finally raising her eyes to her sister's. "You know I can't stand it if you're mad at me. I love you so much."

"Especially when you need money."

"Oh, what a terrible thing to say."

"But that is why you're here, isn't it? To get the money from me?"

"I'll pay you back. I promise. Please, Hailey. She's telling everyone in the office terrible things about me."

Why was it, Hailey wondered, that when she herself cried, she looked like the very devil, with a red nose and blotched cheeks? Ellen looked absolutely gor-geous when she cried. Her eyes shimmered with tears, her lashes clung together wetly, her lips quivered with irresistible vulnerability.

Yet it wasn't out of compassion that Hailey was

going to give her the money. She didn't feel sorry for her sister. She felt only a pity that bordered on disgust. By giving her the money, she would be rid of her, at least temporarily. Hailey didn't want Ellen in her world.

Selfish to the point of neurosis, Ellen would take everything Hailey had to give—money, self-esteem, and, given the chance, Tyler. Scruples wouldn't deter her from taking anything that suited her fancy.

"What's the girl's name?" Hailey asked. "I'll write her a check."

"You can make it out to me."

"What's her name?" Hailey asked sternly, taking her checkbook out of her purse.

Ellen didn't argue, but sulkily supplied the name. Hailey extended the check to her without a word of admonition. Body language said what she was thinking most eloquently. Almost guiltily, Ellen said, "Thank you, Hailey. You're the best sister—"

"I'm the *only* sister, Ellen. And that's the only reason you're here. Don't pretend it's anything else."

"Why are you being so mean all of a sudden?" Ellen asked petulantly.

But Hailey didn't answer her. She was already opening the door, making it clear that now Ellen had what she had come for, she should leave. Tyler was sitting on the living room sofa, one ankle propped on his opposite knee, as he leafed through a magazine.

"Do you realize what a treasure you have in my sister here?" Ellen asked with false affection, coming up to Hailey and hugging her tightly.

"I don't think she realizes it," Tyler said quietly, studying Hailey's shattered face as he rose from the couch.

His words didn't register. All Hailey saw was Ellen folding the check into a neat rectangle and sliding it into the breast pocket of her form-fitting shirt. It was a slow motion gesture, both deliberate and provocative.

"It's been great fun meeting you, Tyler," she said. She went to him, hooked one arm round his neck and drew him down to plant a sisterly kiss on his hard cheek. Hailey saw her sister's lush breasts lightly skim his chest before she pulled away. "Good-bye, Hailey. Thanks." Without another word, she went through the front door. Her footsteps fell like a death knell on Hailey's ears.

She stared at the door for long moments until strong hands settled on her shoulders from behind her. "Hungry yet?"

She became aware of the delicious aroma of cooking steaks, but the thought of eating made her ill. "Yes, I guess so."

"Good, because I'm starved." Tyler kissed her briefly on the back of the neck before turning her and steering her toward the kitchen. "You get everything on the table—which looks lovely, incidentally—and I'll pour the wine. It's opened and breathing now."

He was forcing lightheartedness, trying to pick up where they had left off, when Hailey knew he'd rather be following Ellen out the door. What man would want to be stuck with quartz when he could have a sparkling diamond?

Through dinner he forced conversation on her. He chatted about his plans for Serendipity, complimented her on the idea she had submitted that morning, raved about the food which he was eating with gusto and she was only picking at. She responded desultorily. Why was he carrying on this pretense? Why didn't he just leave? Did he feel sorry for her?

That suspicion began to gnaw on her, and she grew angry and defensive. She didn't need his pity or his sympathy. She didn't want either. Her answers to his persistent questions became more clipped with each passing minute. When he had emptied his parfait glass of the last mouthful of chocolate mousse, she announced that she would clean the kitchen.

He conceded without an argument, but insisted on clearing the table and bringing the dishes to her. It was a wonder any of her china survived. He had left her alone to vent her temper, but she let him know with each slam of a cupboard door, with each rattle of silver, with each ring of clashing china, that she'd just as soon spend the remainder of the evening in solitude.

Snapping out the light in the kitchen, she shoved through the barroom door. Her tantrum was squelched when she saw the scene he had set. A fire was burning in the fireplace. A wine cooler and two clean glasses awaited them on the coffee table in front of the low sofa. The lamps had been drastically dimmed. The drapes on the wide windows had been opened to the jewel-like view of Gatlinburg by night. Tyler was crouched in front of her record collection, selecting a record for the stereo.

"All done?" he asked her over his shoulder when he heard her approach.

"Why did you build a fire?"

"I thought it would be nice, and the evening is cool enough."

"No, I mean why did you bother?"

"No bother."

"Dammit, Tyler, why did you go to the trouble when . . . when . . ."

"When I'm going to be leaving soon?"

She dropped her head and said, "Yes."

"I went to all this trouble because your bad manners and rude behavior aren't going to drive me off, Hailey."

She snapped to attention. Her head came up with a jerk. "Rude—"

"Yes, rude. All through dinner I tried pulling conversation out of you, but you refused to be congenial. And I suppose you always sling things around in your kitchen like a vandal and make a big angry racket while you do the dishes."

"I only assumed—"

"You *assume* a lot of things. In fact that's one of the things you do best—make ridiculous, erroneous assumptions. The latest being that I was going to prefer your big-eyed, big-chested sister to you."

That he had struck on the truth only made her angrier. "You conceited oaf. Do you think I'd care if you did?"

"Yes," he replied calmly. "I think you would, though you certainly never would admit it. The moment she came in this room, you began to chill."

"I was surprised to see her, that's all," Hailey said, flopping down on the couch with studied indifference.

"Uh-huh. You got mad because she came in hanging on to my arm and because we were laughing together. I didn't offer her my arm, she took it. And I was too polite to shake her off. She was laughing because she didn't have anything smarter to do and probably because she knew it would provoke you. And I was laughing because she actually expected me to make a big play for her."

"And you were too polite to do that, too."

He smiled and sank down onto the sofa next to her. "No. I was disinclined. I had the girl I wanted." He reached for her hand and held it snugly. His thumb began stroking lazy circles onto her palm. "Why did you give her the money, Hailey?"

Her eyes went wide. "How did you . . . You listened!?"

"To every word. Why didn't you send her packing? I take it this is not the first time she's hit you for money, or anything she happened to need at the time."

She yanked her hand from him and stood up, going to stand before the hearth. "I can't believe you deliberately invaded my privacy. What gave you the right to eavesdrop on our conversation?" She spun around to face him.

He wasn't in the least perturbed. "I wanted to know what made you change so drastically the minute your sister put in her untimely appearance. Do you always give in to her tears and give her what she wants?"

"Tears aren't the reason—" She broke off abruptly when she realized that she was about to reveal more of herself than was judicious.

"Go on," he said quietly.

"I'm not affected by her tears," Hailey said after a brief pause. "I suppose I give in to her out of habit more than anything else."

"That's a habit you should break, for both your sakes."

"Patterns that are begun during childhood are hard to alter."

"She's always taken advantage of you like that?" Hailey wanted to deny it, but she nodded her head. "That's because she's jealous of you," he said sagely.

She looked at him with incredulity. "*Ellen*, jealous of *me*?" she asked on a high note, then laughed bitterly. "Oh, that's funny. Ellen—beautiful, bouncy Ellen—whom everyone adores, jealous of her stodgy sister."

Tyler leaned far enough forward to take possession of her hand and draw her back onto the sofa, nearer to him this time. He draped an arm around her shoulders and pulled her close.

"Yes. She realized a long time ago that you're

clever, that she couldn't pull the wool over your eyes the way she could with everyone else. You see her for what she is—a silly, selfish creature—and she can't bear that you know the truth about her. So she hurts you."

"And where did you get your diploma, Sigmund?" she asked sarcastically.

He laughed. "You think about it. Sooner or later you'll put your inferiority complex aside and admit that I'm right." Something about the way his fingers were stroking her neck made her want to believe him. Was he telling the truth? Would he rather be with her than Ellen?

"Why did you go in there and twist your hair up?" he asked as his impatient fingers went foraging for the hateful pins. "I told you I liked it loose."

"Ellen looked so tidy and I looked so—"

"Yes, and she had on tight jeans and a shirt bursting at the seams, and you got all uptight and defensive and paranoid as we both know you are inclined to do."

"I did . . . do . . . not," she denied.

"You wilted right before my eyes. Your animation drained away. When I touched you, you tensed, even though just a few minutes earlier you were climbing all over me."

"That's vulgar!" she cried, sitting up and pushing away from him.

"And you love it." He brought her right back, crushing her against the wall of his chest. "That's what's wrong with you, Miss Ashton. Not nearly enough men have talked vulgarly to you. They've been frightened off by this ice palace you've constructed around yourself. Well, I'm too hot-blooded for your green eyes to freeze. I don't give up easily, either. I saw you and I wanted you. I'm going to have you."

With each word his lips had descended closer, until the final word was spoken directly into her mouth. His hands splayed on her back as he drew her to him. Her breasts were flattened against his chest and her nipples flared to life at the igniting touch.

He lowered her down into the cushions in the corner of the sofa. "Would you like some wine?" he asked, his lips sipping at hers.

"Wine?" she asked as though she'd never heard the word before. "No."

"You would love some." He lifted himself from her long enough to fill half a glass with the red wine. He brought it to her mouth and tilted it just enough for one ruby drop to fall upon her lips. Then, before she could drink it, his tongue was there to lick it up. He poured more against her mouth and again he lifted it from her lips and chin with his velvet-rough tongue.

They became intoxicated. Not with the wine, but with each other and the wine-flavored kisses. In his haste to drain the glass, the last bit of wine he dripped onto her lips overflowed and trickled down her cheek. His finger caught it and wiped it away. He was about to lick clean his finger when Hailey captured his hand and lowered it to her mouth. Watching him with half-fearful eyes, she closed her lips around his finger. Her tongue scoured the fingertip, while she sucked on it rhythmically.

"Hailey," he rasped and buried his face in the scented hollow between her breasts. "Do you know what you're doing? Do you have any idea of the passion that hides behind your cool facade?" He placed a hand over her beating heart and her nipple flowered in his palm. His fingers finessed it into a firmer bud.

"Unbutton my shirt," he urged softly. The muscles in his arms bulged as he held himself over her while she carried out the task. When she was done, he rolled to his side so that they were lying face to face on the narrow sofa.

"I want you to get to know me, Hailey. I don't expect you to make love to a stranger."

As if sensing her shyness, he kissed her. His mouth mated with hers in a consciousness-stealing kiss. Imbued with his confidence and strength, she was constrained to put aside her timidity and let her senses direct her.

She started by sifting through the hair lying against the loose collar of his shirt. Then she explored his ears with a touch of her fingers. She pulled away from his kiss to smooth his brows, which seemed to be in a perpetually ruffled state. His eyes remained closed as she traced the patrician length of his nose to his upper lip. He kissed her fingertips in turn as they skated across his lips.

Adjusting her gentle curves to his hard body, she kissed his throat, bravely letting her tongue investigate that deep triangle at its base. Her fingers combed through the crisp hair on his chest and marveled at the mysterious mounds and ridges beneath his warm skin.

Accidentally her fingers brushed across his nipple. His sharp intake of breath and the sudden stiffening of his body alarmed her. She snatched her hand away. He lay perfectly still, in an attitude of breathless anticipation.

As though drawn by a magnet, her fingers returned to that place on his chest. Hesitantly, she touched it with her middle finger. Ring finger. Index finger, circling him slowly. The turgid skin grew tighter. She circled it again.

"Oh sweetheart," he groaned and tilted her head back to kiss her with unleashed passion. Recklessly, he sought the hem of her top. His anxious hands drew it over her head and flung it away. His mouth worked its way down her chest. He pulled one black satin strap away and rained deliciously damp kisses on her shoulder. Lower. And lower still.

Just when she expected him to rid her of the camisole, he smoothed the lace over her breasts with gentle hands and pulled it taut. The heat of his eyes licked her like live flame as he savored the picture of her nipples straining against the black lace. He could have been photographing her, so intense was his look.

Then he kissed her. His tongue raked across her nipple with a delving motion that the veil of lace only intensified. His lips surrounded her and squeezed her gently. Reflexively, her hips ground against him, feeling his growing desire.

"Oh yes, Hailey, my love. Yes."

His hand on the curve of her hips held her against him for long moments while their bodies pulsated together. Slowly, painstakingly, his hands slipped between them, found the fastening of her slacks, and unzipped them.

He pressed his palm over her navel and rotated it in time to a sensual cadence. His fingers smoothed down the naked skin of her abdomen until he encountered the lacy band of her panties. Hooking his fingers under it, he dared to discover what lay beyond.

His touch was all the more hypnotic for its featherlike lightness. Unbearable heat consumed her as she experienced his persuasion. Heartbeats thundered through her veins and between her thighs until she arched against the hand that had brought on this blissful malady.

"You're beautiful," he whispered when his fingers found her pliant and moist. Then he touched her in such an erotic, forbidden way that she went rigid with shock.

"Tyler," she cried in dismay, pushing away from

him with frantic hands. It was a revealing reaction, as astonishing to him as his touch had been to her.

He raised himself over her. His gray eyes bored into her wide, frightened green ones, silently asking if the unbelievable were true. "Hailey?" His little finger lifted a disobedient curl from her cheek and replaced it in the mass that spread out behind her head like a fan. "Am I the first?"

Unable to meet his penetrating stare, she squeezed her eyes shut and turned her head away, pressing her cheek against the cushion of the sofa. "I'm a freak. I tried to tell you I wasn't made for this. You wouldn't believe me."

Touched by the misery in her voice, he raised his index finger to stroke her cheek as one does an infant's, with tenderness, almost in fear of bringing unintentional pain. "No. You are not a freak. You are a very special woman. So special that I'm humbled and to no small degree awed by you."

She opened her eyes, but hadn't the courage to look at him. She couldn't believe she had heard him correctly. Ridicule, rebuke, perhaps even laughter were what she had expected. She hadn't expected the low, reverent gentle quality in his voice.

"Don't attach any mystical importance to this," she said defensively. "It only means that no one has wanted me before."

He did laugh then, a deep rumbling sound in his chest that never quite made it to his lips. "You're a virgin in more ways than one, Hailey. You're terribly naive about how men see you. And I for one am damned glad. I won't have to be constantly fighting them off."

She found the courage to look at him. The corners of his mouth were lifted into a tender smile. His eyes were warm as they scanned her face. "You still want me?" She didn't consider the irony of the question. Whereas before she had insisted they would never be lovers, now his answer to her question was of utmost importance to her.

He dropped a light kiss on her lips. "I want you more than ever. So much that I ache," he said ruefully. "But I would never hurt you, Hailey. I would never distress you in any way. Tonight, you've been put through several major emotional upheavals. Not very conducive to making love. When the time is right, we'll both know it. I go after what I want. I usually get it. But I've found that the longer I have to wait for something, the more I value it."

He drew her into a sitting position, helped her refasten her slacks, and pulled her top over her head. As he was buttoning his shirt he said, "The park closes Sunday night. Early Monday morning, you, Faith, and I are going on a vacation."

"What?"

"We're going to get away from it all."

"I can't leave the day after the park closes. There are a million things that have to be done."

"You are Director of Guest Relations. When all the guests are gone, who are you going to relate to?" She took a moment to admire his mouth as he smiled, then she forced herself back to the subject.

"I have group tours to book for next season. Promotional campaigns to outline. Brochures to lay out. Tickets—"

"All of which can wait awhile. We're going. I have a cabin on Fontana Lake. Be ready early Monday morning."

"I'm not going, Tyler."

CHAPTER | 8

"I'm not going, Tyler."

"We'll pick you up at eight. And if you're not out of bed, I'll come in and drag you out."

"I'm not going, Tyler."

"You sound like a broken record."

Indeed, she did. All week she had been repeating the words and all week he had been dismissing them. Ever since he had first mentioned the trip to Fontana Lake in North Carolina, she had been telling him that she wasn't going. Excuse after excuse had been offered, but he had negated them all with the glad-heartedness with which he was doing everything these days.

The last week of Serendipity's season was a hectic one for each employee. Adding to the general chaos, Tyler was a visible force in the park. He showed up at the oddest times, in the most unusual places, making supervisors nervous and anxiety-ridden. However, he seemed pleased with the park's operation. One evening over dinner he confided to Hailey that he and Faith had come to the park many times.

"Until we ran into an ornery bee, I was treated like any other guest. Since everything seemed to be running well, I didn't interfere with Sanders's management. However"—his eyes shone with devilish glee—"it never hurts for the boss to make his presence known."

Hailey was busy taking questionnaires and computing the results. The comments were generally favorable at this time of the year, for the crowds had thinned out considerably, and each guest could enjoy the park at a more relaxed pace.

During the winter, she would compile a thorough report from the questionnaires taken throughout the summer and submit it to Harmon Sanders. From this official report, each department could analyze its performance and concentrate on the trouble spots.

She was grateful for the work she had to do that week in conjunction with the park's closing. Were it not for that to occupy her mind, she would have had to deal with her conflicting feelings concerning Tyler Scott.

He spoke with her several times a day on the telephone, and it alarmed her to realize that she began to look forward to those intrusions. He was continually popping into her office on one pretext or another. Hailey hoped that his attention wasn't being noticed, but apparently it was. She was barraged by questions.

"What's Mr. Scott going to do about enlarging the parking lot?"

"What's Mr. Scott going to put in that area they're clearing out?"

She always knew the answers, too, and that in itself was a clue as to how interwoven their lives had become. He often used her as a sounding board for his ideas. Her opinion was valued. He asked for her suggestions and weighed them carefully.

She had dinner with him and Faith every night. It had almost become a matter of form. One night, after an especially arduous day, they treated themselves to a swim in the pool at the Glenstone. One evening they cooked hamburgers on Hailey's outdoor grill. Another night they stayed in the park until it closed and, under duress, Hailey rode the Sidewinder for the first time.

Much to Hailey's relief, Tyler wasn't as overt in his sexual pursuit as he had been. Or was she relieved? Each time she caught him watching her, the flame of desire in his eyes was all too evident and never failed to kindle a response in her.

Yet he treated her like a friendly companion. He touched her often and openly, but courteously, not sensuously. She denied the vague disappointment she felt each evening when he kissed her good night with brotherly fondness and nothing more.

Only once during the week did he let her know that, far from cooling, his desire was simmering dangerously close to the surface.

He had called her office early one morning and asked her to meet him at the Cave. "Hurry, before the park opens. I want to tell you about an idea I have."

She rushed through the employees' compound and within minutes was at the turnstile of the popular ride. Round wooden tubs took a water route through a man-made cave in which animated characters cavorted, frightening and entertaining spectators. The Cave was well-frequented during the summertime because it provided a respite from the heat. And it was especially popular with teenagers because its cool interior was dark and conducive to romance.

Tyler was waiting for her at the entrance of the ride, chatting amiably with the young woman who was operating it. "Good morning, Miss Ashton," he said, tongue-in-cheek, when she approached.

"Good morning, Mr. Scott," she replied. "What did you want to see me about?"

"I have an idea that needs your sound judgment. I've told Linda not to let anyone in until we come out." Instead of getting into one of the tubs that were towed by underwater cables through the shallow canal, he opened a camouflaged door to let them into the interior workings of the ride. He switched on a flashlight as he pulled Hailey through the door.

"Do you know where you're going and what you're doing?" she asked warily as he led her into the stygian darkness.

"Sure. I checked it out yesterday. Just stay on the path. Oh, and be sure to watch for spiders."

"Spiders!" she shrieked.

He laughed as he squeezed her hand. "Only kidding. The kids who work in this place traipse through here like it was nothing. But do watch your head. Some of the overhead beams are low." They walked around the motorized miniature men who were eerily still now. "The word around the compound is that this is a terrific place to take your coffee break."

"You're kidding," Hailey said. "Why would anyone want to come in here unless it was absolutely necessary?"

"To watch lovers making out. You'd be surprised what two innovative people can do in those tubs. The ride takes seven minutes. A lot of frustration can be worked off in seven minutes."

Hailey was laughing in spite of herself. "I don't believe any of this. Who told you?"

"Well, they didn't actually *tell* me. I overheard two of the boys talking in the wardrobe room the other day. I came in here yesterday to see for myself, and they were right. It's quite a sideshow!"

He stopped to face her now. The flashlight was held down at his side, giving them a dim circle of illumination. "So let me guess your great idea," she said saucily. "You want to sell tickets to lecherous old men to come in here and watch teenagers neck."

He snapped his fingers loudly. "That's even better than the one I had." He laughed then and embraced her in a bear hug. "Actually, I was thinking of something to cool people off rather than to warm them up."

"It's already cool in here."

"But I want to make it cooler."

"How?"

"I was in a shopping center in Dallas last year at Christmas. Every hour on the hour, for about five minutes, it snowed!"

"Snowed? You mean—"

"Yes. No matter what the weather was like, great big flakes of snow would fall on the whole mall area. They had this machine that made the snow and blew it out. So here's my idea. I'd like to revamp this ride. Take out the stuff that's been in here for several years and put in a snowscape. Have our merry little men building snowmen, skiing, etc., and—"

"Have one of the machines snowing on the people as they ride through!"

"You're always three steps ahead of me," he said. "What do you think?"

"I love it."

"Really? You wouldn't just say that because you know it's what I want to hear?"

"No. I think it'll be something different. People will talk about it and everyone will want to come see it. You're a genius, Mr. Scott."

"That's true, but I try to stay humble." He got an elbow in the ribs as he propelled her back toward the door. "Ouch! It's expected of me to carry on the family tradition. My father was an extremely astute businessman."

"Was? He's dead?"

"No, very much alive. I just meant 'was' in the sense that he's retired. On my thirtieth birthday, he turned the whole kit and caboodle over to me. He and Mom live in Atlanta."

"You really are a business whiz kid, though, aren't you?"

He didn't answer for a while and she could almost feel his shrug in the darkness. "I've been lucky on some gambles that paid off." It was obvious by his tone that he didn't want to talk about his financial success, so she didn't press the issue.

"Mom and Dad would like you. I want you to meet them soon. Have I ever told you that whenever I look at your legs I get turned on?"

She stumbled in the dark. "You can't even see them."

"Yes I can. I'm holding the light on them."

"Well you ought to be watching where you're going."

Just as the words were out of her mouth, she heard the sickening crack of bone against wood. Tyler cursed loudly and dropped the flashlight, which rolled in a half-circle before coming to rest against his shoe.

"Oh, Tyler," she moaned, covering her mouth with her hand. "What did you do?"

He made a grating sound. "I ran into one of those damn low beams I warned you about. Dammit. That hurts."

"Let me see," she said gently, coming up on her toes and easing his hand away from his forehead. Because of the darkness, she gingerly felt along his brow until she found the hard lump forming on his temple. "I'm so sorry," she said in a crooning, soothing voice. With delicate fingers, she examined the injury. "I think it'll be all right. It's swelling and that's a good sign. It's when it doesn't swell that it can be dangerous."

"Never mind about that now," he said in a low growl as he pulled her against him. He sought her mouth.

"Tyler, your head—"

"Hurts like hell. Kiss me and take my mind off it."

He kissed her with such urgency that for a moment she was too stunned to respond. His tongue was a sweet invader, a plunderer in her mouth that gave more than it took. His hands were those of a sculptor, molding her malleable body to his. With a suggestion of desperation, his hips rubbed against her.

Whether it was their discussion about the clandestine loving that went on in the Cave, or the darkness that enveloped them, or his touch that she had missed, something prompted her to answer his provocative movement with one of her own.

"Oh God, Hailey." With a shuddering effort, he imposed restraint on his body. His lips blazed across her cheek to her ear. "You're sweet medicine. But I've only exchanged one dull ache for another. This one will surely kill me."

"I'm sorry," she whispered. She wanted to sound contrite, but he heard the smile behind her words.

"Um. I'll bet you are. I think you derive a perverse delight from torturing me like this." He captured her earlobe with his teeth and worried it gently. "Your time's coming, Miss Ashton. You'll be panting for my lovemaking, and I'll make you purr with contentment."

Embarrassed because she knew he was probably right, she knelt down to pick up the flashlight. The tunnel was suddenly ablaze with light.

"Wha—" She stared in stupefaction at Tyler's hand near a wall light switch. Her green eyes narrowed to suspicious slits as she turned to glare at his sly expression. "You knew there were lights in here all along. Why didn't you turn them on when we first came in?"

He grinned wolfishly. "Now why do you think? There's something to be learned from the younger generation."

"Oh," she fumed. She spun away from him and, with the advantage of light, easily made her way back to the secret door. He was chuckling in satisfaction as he followed her.

At the exit, he murmured only loud enough for her to hear, "You're on borrowed time, Hailey. You'll be in my bed before we get back from Fontana."

"I'm not going, Tyler," she had said then. He had only laughed.

And he was laughing now three days later, as he carelessly leaned against the railing around her deck. "You're going. I've had someone in to clean the cabin, stock the pantry and refrigerator, and spruce up the place just for you. You're going."

"We closed the park to the public today, but there's still so much I have to do."

"Am I going to have to fire you to get you away from there?"

"You wouldn't dare."

"You're right. But you're going with Faith and me tomorrow. That's why I insisted you come home early tonight. Pack, get a good night's sleep, and we'll pick you up at eight." He kissed her soundly and left confident that she was going with them.

And of course she was.

Arguing with herself the whole while she was packing, she tried to talk herself out of going. He had promised that he would complete his seduction while they were away. Why, then, was she going with him? She waltzed around the answer to that until she could deny it no longer. She wanted to be seduced.

The risks involved in having such an affair were too numerous to count. No man had ever been worth those risks before. Until Tyler. She had been attracted to him from the moment she saw him. He had changed her. She wasn't the same person she had been before meeting him. Her life was different. No matter what the stakes, she wanted to savor the magic he had brought into her world for as long as it lasted.

What joy had she known before him? He had barreled into her life with the impetus of a steamroller and hadn't let up for one moment. And though she had fought him in self-defense, she had secretly relished the excitement he had introduced into her staid, stale existence.

On the one hand, she had resented his overbearing

manner, and on the other, she had welcomed it. Competence and self-reliance were admirable traits, but they were also tiresome. Tyler had showed her that vulnerability had its merits, too. Privately, she confessed to loving the way his hands and mouth reduced her to womanhood in its purest form. She *wanted* to be a woman for Tyler Scott.

He had treated her to more affection than she had ever had. He had brought her to a higher plane of emotional response than she could ever have guessed she was capable of. She wanted to lie submissively in Tyler's bed and know the culmination of all his seductive promises.

She had only a moment's trepidation before she fell asleep. *Was* she doing the right thing? Did it *matter* if it was right? All her life she had done as she was expected to, striving not to disappoint anyone. She had performed as others dictated that she should. Where had circumspection gotten her?

Her parents had died weeping because Ellen wasn't with them. Her sister "loved" her only when she needed her. One can only win so many silver medals for good conduct before they tarnish and become worthless. For once Hailey Ashton was going to do what *she* wanted, right or wrong, and damn the consequences.

"I've never had a picnic in a river before," Hailey said, biting the crunchy crust off a piece of fried chicken. They had stopped at a carry-out restaurant to pick up their lunch before leaving Gatlinburg.

"I think we're real pioneers," Tyler said as he leaned back on his elbows. Surrounding them was the swirling white water of the Little Pigeon River. They had taken the winding two-lane highway through the Great Smoky Mountains National Park toward the North Carolina state line. When they became hungry and began looking for a picnic spot, Tyler had pulled the car into one of the scenic rest areas along the highway.

Rather than settle for the mundane, he had suggested that they eat their lunch in the river on one of the large, flat rocks that littered the riverbed. Brushing aside their cautious protests, he had led Hailey and Faith from one rock to another until they reached the largest and most level. As usual, he had gotten his way. And, as usual, he had been right. It was delightful.

"I've never been on any kind of picnic before," Faith said, munching on her drumstick.

Hailey and Tyler stared at the girl in dismay, looked at each other, and then back at Faith. "Of course you must have, Faith," Tyler said gently.

"I don't think so," she said, matter-of-factly. "Unless it was before I can remember. Mommy never took me on one. She didn't even like to eat on the patio because she said it was a lot of trouble and she didn't like bugs. Once my Brownie troop went on an all day camp-out, but I had the chicken pox and couldn't go. No, I think this is my first picnic." She seemed totally unaffected by this deficiency in her childhood, and that made it all the more pathetic.

"Well, this is certainly not the last," Tyler said and tugged on her pigtail. "From now on, we'll have all the picnics you can stand."

"Can Hailey come on all of them?" Faith asked.

Tyler turned laughing eyes on Hailey and struck a pose of deep concentration. "I don't know," he said, slowly stroking his chin. "Do you think we ought to ask her?"

Caught up in the game, Faith giggled. "It might hurt her feelings if we don't."

"Well then, I guess we will." He sat up and pulled an embarrassed Hailey between his raised knees, drawing her back against his chest. He nuzzled her ear with his nose. The display of familiarity in front of Faith surprised Hailey, but it felt right, comfortable.

"Oh, Daddy, gross," Faith said in exasperation.

"You think this is gross, huh? Watch this." He tilted Hailey's head back and kissed her with comical passion, grinding his mouth over hers.

Faith was overcome by giggles. "That's just the way they kiss on TV."

Tyler was laughing with his daughter. Hailey was smiling as she leaned against him. "Just what have you been watching on TV, young lady? We'll have to monitor that from now on," Tyler said to Hailey. *We*. It sounded so permanent. She snuggled closer.

"I'm never going to let anyone kiss me like that!"

Faith said firmly. "No one will want to, but I wouldn't let him anyway."

"Oh yes, you will, and I'll want to shoot the first boy brave enough to try it," Tyler said.

"Why?" Faith asked.

"Why? Because you're *my* girl, that's why."

She blushed prettily and looked down at her sneakers. "Well, no boys will want to kiss me, so you won't have to worry."

"Plenty of boys will want to. You're the prettiest girl around."

She jerked her head up to stare at her father. "Do you *really* think so?"

"Of course I do. You're the prettiest girl I've ever seen. I've always thought so, ever since I picked you out at the hospital."

"Daddy, I know you didn't pick me out. I know where babies come from." She spoke in a disparaging voice, but Hailey knew the girl was glowing with happiness under Tyler's flattery.

Hailey wanted to turn around and hug him. Faith's self-esteem had improved in the past few weeks. Hailey thought she might have contributed to that in a small measure, but the credit really went to Tyler. He spoke to the girl differently, no longer dismissing her as a child, but treating her like a person. The result of his attention was readily apparent. Faith had opened up like a flower who had been waiting a long time for spring.

"Why don't you pick up the remains of our picnic?"

he asked of his daughter. "That may earn you a dollar or two."

"Okay," she said eagerly.

As she went about the task, Hailey laid her head against his shoulder and looked up at him. He was bending so close over her that his breath was a warm vapor against her face. She could distinguish each eyelash. The dark centers of his eyes mirrored the invitation in hers. Answering that beckoning expression, his mouth came down to cover her lips.

This kiss wasn't for anyone's amusement. It was entirely selfish and shared only by them. It wasn't passionate. Neither of them was an exhibitionist; neither felt it was proper to give way to passion before Faith's impressionable eyes.

But it was a puissant kiss, rife with longing, unquenched desire, and quiet understanding. Sweetly, his tongue nudged the tip of hers, yet he could have been touching her in a much more intimate place for the impact the gesture had. That secret core deep inside her exploded and showered her body with sparks of sensation. What appeared chaste on the outside was most wanton within.

He raised his head and Hailey saw the desire burning in his eyes, a desire matching the smoldering coal of her own need. He helped her stand. Weakened by the onslaught of passion he had aroused, she swayed against him. His arms came around her protectively. He knew, understood, and shared her weakness. For precious long moments, they clung together.

When at last they released each other, Faith was eyeing them keenly. Her braces were fully revealed by her wide grin, and in her gray eyes, so like her father's, a newfound happiness was dancing.

They arrived at Fontana Lake late in the afternoon, having taken their time driving through the National Park and enjoying the sights along the way. The forested mountains, with the gray blue mist—that gave them their name—shrouding their peaks, were tinted with the vivid hues of autumn.

Faith had complained about her restricted view, until Tyler relented and allowed her to sit in the front seat with him and Hailey. As it turned out, everyone enjoyed the arrangement. Faith, because she could see more through the wide front windshield. And Tyler and Hailey because they were forced to sit touching from knee to shoulder.

It seemed that Tyler's right arm was inordinately busy as he drove, never remaining still for long. It finally occurred to Hailey that every time he moved it, it brushed across her left breast, keeping her in a state of constant agitation. When she turned her head to look at him accusingly, he grinned down at her mischievously and laughed. His wink congratulated her on finally catching on to his cleverness. Justice was served when she punished him by placing her hand high on his thigh.

His "cabin" turned out to be a three-bedroom, three-bath dwelling larger than most houses. The living room opened onto a view of the lake, while each bedroom had a vista of the mountains. It was thoroughly and tastefully furnished and equipped with all the amenities.

After showering and changing their clothes, they drove to a nearby lodge for dinner. Returning to the house, Faith informed them by quoting from the *TV Guide* that "the most terrifying motion picture ever filmed" was on that night.

"We can't miss that, can we?" Tyler teased.

Faith put on a nightgown with Snoopy and Woodstock on its front and stretched out on the floor in front of the television screen to await the movie. She soon became engrossed in a musical special featuring one of her favorite rock stars.

"Let's get comfortable, too," Tyler said to Hailey, going toward his bedroom and peeling his sweater over his head as he walked.

Hailey closed the door to the bedroom that had been designated as hers, a room that was decorated in myriad shades of yellow and gold. She took off the skirt and blouse she had worn to dinner and hung them in the closet. Stripping down to her panties, she put on a long satin robe. It had been an extravagant birthday present from Ellen that she had never had an occasion to wear before. Its rich, dark green fabric highlighted the color of her hair and contributed to the brilliance of her eyes. An invisible zipper closed the garment from her neck to her knees, and the sleeves belled in a wide hem just below her elbows.

She was searching her suitcase for her slippers when there was a discreet knock on her door. "Who is it?" she asked breathlessly, quickly dousing herself with perfume.

"A naked savage bent on satisfying his lust."

She was laughing as she pulled open the door. "You liar. You're not naked at all."

"Give me five seconds," he said, backing her into the room. He had on a pair of gray warm-up pants and an Atlanta Falcons sweatshirt.

"You're crazy."

"And getting crazier," he murmured as he tried to capture her mouth. "You're driving me crazy." He succeeded in trapping her lips against his. He parted them agilely and kissed her with the savagery he had intimated. His tongue sank into her mouth, instinctively finding the most sensitive places and playing havoc with her senses.

"Tyler—"

"Want has become need, Hailey. I need you."

Pushing away from him, she sobbed softly, "We can't." Then as she ducked her head and stared at her bare feet she said hoarsely, "*I* can't."

"I know."

She had thought he would curse, beg, shout, but never concur. This quiet agreement was the most surprising of a long list of astonishing statements. "You . . . you *know*?" She could barely mouth the words.

"Faith."

Her features softened with emotion. He was coming to know how she felt about things. She nodded, touching his face with hands that told him how much his understanding was appreciated.

"We're adults, Hailey. We know what it's about, but she doesn't. I can't preach to her about morality if—"

"I understand, Tyler. I *do*. I was hoping you would."

His index finger came up to trace her bottom lip. "You understand everything." He spoke so softly the words were almost indistinct, yet she heard him. "But do you understand what it's like for a man to want a woman as much as I want you? I've put you in every conceivable erotic fantasy. I ache, Hailey."

"So do I."

Her words stunned him. In disbelieving wonder, he stared at her as her fingers closed around the tassel on the zipper of her robe. Their eyes remained locked as the zipper rasped through the rustling fabric. The sound was amplified a thousand times over in the still room. Tyler didn't move, didn't breathe.

When the robe was opened, she reached for his hand, brought it to her mouth, and kissed his palm. Knowing she might never have the courage again, she drew his hand to the top curve of her breast and pressed it against her soft flesh. Her palm caressed the back of his hand, his knuckles, his strong, tapering fingers.

"Hailey," he said in a voice rough with emotion. His eyes dropped from hers to fall on what seemed to come to life under the tender manipulation of his fingers. They combed down the roundness of her breast to the dusky center. His fingers marveled over her and he watched in awe as she responded. His eyes were lifted to hers once more before he lowered his head to cherish with his mouth what his hand had prepared for him.

His tongue laved her nipples with long, circling, sensuous strokes. Lips firm and moist closed around them. Ever so gently, he suckled her. She whispered his name and slipped her hands beneath his sweatshirt to caress the furred skin of his chest.

Tyler was seized by a surging desire that he forced down by a sheer act of will. He encompassed her with possessive arms. His hard, hot cheek nestled against the softness of her breasts. "It will be so good, Hailey," he vowed in a harsh whisper. "It will be so good."

He kissed her, not allowing them to touch anywhere except on the lips that molded together as though by design. They smiled at each other with new tenderness when they reluctantly pulled apart. They had just restored their clothing when Faith called from the living room. "Daddy, Hailey, the movie's starting."

By the second commercial, Faith was curled up beside Tyler on the deep sofa, burying her face in his shoulder during each gory scene. He kept an arm firmly around Hailey, and each time he looked at her, his eyes echoed the promise he had made.

CHAPTER 9

Breakfast was a boisterous affair, with Tyler acting as chef and Hailey and Faith issuing him orders. Somehow, despite all the confusion, the pancakes and bacon got on the table.

Hailey was impressed by the furnishings in the house. The kitchen was well equipped. None of the rooms had that sterile quality that is inherent in houses infrequently opened and aired. How often did Tyler come here? Had he and Monica ever come here together? She doubted it. It was too new for them to have used it during their married life, which had ended ten years ago.

Was this his getaway, where he escaped from the pressures of the business world? Had he brought other women here? How many?

"What's on your mind, Red?"

She was brought out of her disturbing musings by Tyler's question. She had been vacantly staring into her coffee cup and hadn't realized that Faith had deserted the messy kitchen for the television set. "Nothing," she answered in a way invariably annoying to men.

He didn't take umbrage. "I'll tell you what was on *my* mind," he said with a leer as he leaned across the cluttered table to take her hand.

"I *know* what was on your mind," she said, trying to maintain her severe expression.

"Guilty. Ever since I collided with a tall, sexy, red-haired lady with glittering green eyes, my mind has been in the gutter. So I plead guilty. Bind my hands and feet with chains. Flay me with whips. I deserve only the cruelest and most unusual punishment."

"Stop!" she cried, laughing. "You sound like you're into S and M."

"Not yet, but I never knock anything until I've tried it." He was smiling, revealing the strong white teeth which she knew were capable of executing delicious torture. But as she watched, his teasing manner diminished and the fingers caressing her hand concentrated all their energy into the thumb that massaged her palm. "I'm guilty of many things, Hailey, but not of having a parade of women marching through my life."

Every feature of her face contributed to her look of dismay. Uncanny. His perception of her thoughts was uncanny. "That *was* what you were speculating on, wasn't it?" he asked. "How many women I've brought here or had torrid affairs with?"

She lowered her eyes. "It's none of my business."

He tugged on her hand. "Look at me, Hailey," he commanded, and she obeyed. She didn't want to know, but she had to. "Since my divorce, my encounters with women have been few, brief, and dismal. I have never pursued a woman with the diligence I have pursued you."

"No?" She needed so badly to believe him.

"No. I've never let a woman come between me and business. On that trip I took recently, I crammed two weeks' work into one because I couldn't stand being away from you."

Her temples were throbbing, not only from his words, but the definitive way in which he spoke them. To cover her emotional response, she stood quickly and began to clear the table with clammy, clumsy hands.

"Normally, when I sit in important, decision-making business meetings I concentrate on nothing except the subject under discussion. Do you know what I've been doing in all the business meetings I've attended since I met you?"

"We really need to get this cleaned—"

He caught her busy hands with his and drew her against him, trapping her hands between their bodies. "I've been thinking about you. About how we must take a trip to the coast so we can make love in the ocean. I want to stand with you in the surf and watch the waves lapping at your breasts."

"Tyler—"

"And in my mind I must have taken a thousand showers with you, soaping every inch of you and then having you return the favor. I know exactly what you feel like under lathered hands."

Her hands had opened and flattened against his chest. Now she placed her forehead against his breastbone and shook her head. "You embarrass me, Tyler. You really shouldn't talk to me like this."

His mouth was moving in her hair. "Would you rather we skip the talking stage and move right on to the action?" Her breath was released in a half-sigh, half-laugh. Cupping her face between his palms, he tilted her head back. "Worry about something else, Hailey, but don't worry about other women."

He kissed her then, sliding his hand under the waistband of her jeans and curving it to the shape of her hips. His mouth was ardent, insistent, persuasive, and for the remainder of the day, she didn't worry about anything.

Tyler rented a motorboat and they spent the hours of the morning on the lake. By noon, windblown, exhilarated, and ravenous, they were demolishing cheeseburgers, french fries, and onion rings at a local hangout.

"What can we do now?" Faith asked as she dipped the last french fry into the catsup on her plate.

Tyler and Hailey groaned in unison. "Take a nap," he said hopefully.

"Oh, come on. Let's go horseback riding. Or hiking. I think they have motorcycles you can rent someplace."

She settled for hiking, then a rousing game of table tennis in the lodge that was made available to property owners. While Tyler and Hailey were recovering from a five-game match, Faith played the electronic games. She met another girl her age who was just as addicted. In the end, she had to be dragged away from both her new friend and the machines.

By the time they returned to the house, they were all exhausted. "I suggest," Tyler said, "that we rest before dinner. We'll go eat barbecue at that place that has the Country-Western band."

The ladies agreed to that and they all retired to their rooms to recuperate from the day's activities. Hailey bathed leisurely in the deep tub and reapplied her makeup. She let her hair hang free and it curled around her face and neck beguilingly.

She dressed in a dark plaid cotton skirt characteristic of the "prairie look." Her blouse was Victorian, having a round yoke across the chest and shoulders. A high, ruffle-edged collar reached to her jawline. The hemline of her skirt covered the tops of her soft leather boots.

The buttons on the back of her blouse had given her trouble, so she had asked Faith to help. "Gee, you look beautiful, Hailey," she said as she admired her idol.

"Thank you. I was just about to tell you the same. Is that a new outfit?"

"Yes," Faith said proudly, showing off a new shirt and a bright blue overall with cuffs that banded her ankles. "Do you like it? Daddy bought it for me, but I had to talk him into it. He said he'd never seen pants like this."

"Well, he'd better start looking through your fashion magazines, right?"

"Right," Faith giggled as they went to join her father.

"What's so funny?" he asked.

"Nothing a man could understand," Hailey said breezily. "It was girl talk." Faith giggled harder at his scowl.

The restaurant was crowded and noisy, but everyone was having a good time. The dance floor resembled a boxing ring where couples were jostling each other to the beat of the music. What the band lacked in technique, it more than made up for in volume.

They were finishing up their meal when Faith jumped out of her chair and yelled, "Hey, Kim!" She waved her arms to the girl being seated halfway across the room. "That's my friend," she said hastily to Tyler and Hailey before she ran through the maze of tables to speak to her new acquaintance.

Hailey and Tyler watched and, after a brief interchange, Faith was leading Kim and her mother back to their table.

"Hello," the woman said pleasantly, over the din of the restaurant. "I'm Frances Harper. My daughter Kim met your daughter in the lodge this afternoon. They got on so well and had such a good time, I wondered if you'd let Faith sleep over at our house tonight."

Faith and Kim, who was plumper by several pounds

and shorter by several inches than Faith, were clutching hands, hopping up and down, barely able to contain their anxiety that permission might not be granted.

Now Faith spoke, "Pl-eeee-ze. She has Atari on her television, and that new album I've been wanting, and I'll be nice, I promise. Pl-eeee-ze."

The adults laughed at her earnestness. "You'd be doing me a favor to let her come," Mrs. Harper said. "My husband and I enjoy rest and relaxation when we come up here. I'm afraid it gets boring for Kim, especially when we have to take her out of school like we did this time. This was the only week my husband could get off.

"We live on the same road as you in the red brick colonial. She'll be no trouble and I'll watch them carefully."

Mrs. Harper was speaking mainly to Hailey, as though she would be making the decision. Suddenly it occurred to her that the woman naturally assumed she was Faith's mother. "I know you would . . ." she hedged. What could she say?

"I don't see any reason why she can't go, do you, Hailey?" Tyler asked. From the tone of his voice and the familiarity with which he placed his hand on her shoulder, she could very well be his wife and Faith's mother.

"No. I think it'll be all right."

"Oh, thank you," both girls gushed at the same time. "Thank you, thank you," Faith said as she kissed both Tyler and Hailey in turn. Then the two excited girls rushed off to join Mr. Harper who had remained at the table.

"Kim has extra pajamas, so we'll just take Faith with us from here."

"We'll pick her up sometime in the morning," Tyler said. "Thank you for asking her."

"Thank you for letting her come. It was nice to meet you, both. I'll see you in the morning." She went back to her own table.

Hailey's spirit had suffered a mortal wound. It was obvious that Mrs. Harper had taken them to be husband and wife. But she wasn't Tyler's wife. Not by a long shot. What was she to him? A companion for the weekend? A bed partner until he tired of her? "Few, brief, and dismal." Those were the words he had used to describe his affairs with women. But were they accurate ones? Would he be repeating those words to the next woman he wanted, making her feel special? Seducing her?

"Hailey?"

"I'm sorry." At the sound of his voice she blinked up at him. "What did you say?"

"I asked if you were finished. Would you like anything else?"

"No, I'm fine."

"Let's go then."

They weaved their way toward the front door. Faith waved and threw kisses to them from the Harpers' table, where she was sitting politely while they ate their dinner.

"Are you cold?" Tyler asked her as they were walking toward the parked car. At the touch of his hand on the back of her neck, she had shivered.

"Yes, a little."

"I'll build a fire when we get home."

Home?

She sat stiffly by his side and they didn't speak during the short drive to his sprawling house. Walking toward the front door, he clasped her hand in his and swung them back and forth. "A harvest moon. Look at the reflection on the lake."

The moon's image on the lake was indeed beautiful, but Hailey didn't want to see it. She didn't want the night to lend itself to romance. Faith's presence had kept them apart last night. Faith wasn't here tonight. Who would protect her from his seduction? Would she have to rely on herself to resist him? If that were the case, God help her.

Tyler hung his corduroy sport coat on a hall tree after closing the front door behind them. "I stacked the fire while I was waiting for you and Faith to get dressed. I only need to light it."

"Good."

"Do you want some coffee? Wine? Anything?"

"No."

"Are you sure? There's still some of that delicious Chablis left. One small glass?"

"No."

From his squatting position in front of the fireplace

he turned around and looked up at her. "Cat got your
tongue?"

"No."

He laughed then and pushed himself up. Flames
were curling around the kindling he had piled under
the logs. "All your words put together since we left the
restaurant wouldn't make a simple sentence." He came
to her and squeezed her shoulders gently. "You
shouldn't worry about it, you know."

Her dark lashes lifted from her anguished green
eyes as she looked up at him. "Shouldn't worry about
what?"

"That Mrs. Harper mistook you for my wife. It was
a natural mistake, Hailey."

"Yes. And she will reach a natural conclusion about
me when she finds out I'm not."

"When are you going to stop letting what other people think dictate what you do, and let your own in-
stincts guide you?"

She pulled away from him and went to stand at the
wide windows. The tears in her eyes made the silver
reflection on the water even more ethereal. The cool
October wind bent the trees to graceful angles. The
stars were spectacular jewels undimmed by city
lights. It was a beautiful night, a display of nature in
its most primitive and basic state. She wanted to be-
long to it.

Tyler had asked her the question she had asked herself.

Why should she care what anyone thought of her affair with him? What did she have to lose? Loneliness. Boredom. A life without depth or color or love. Any kind of love.

She turned back to him slowly. The tears dried before they could be shed, but not before they made her eyes luminescent. Moonlight shone on her hair while firelight danced across her face.

He was what she wanted. Tall, hard, powerful, intelligent, humorous. His hair lay in dark, sculpted waves. From under thick brows, his gray eyes glowed as he looked at her. His pose was casual—one shoulder leaning against the mantel—but Hailey knew the latent strength beneath the tanned skin.

"I think maybe I will have some wine," she said.

"I'll have some, too. Will you pour? I want to get something out of the bedroom."

When she came back into the living room carrying a tray with two glasses and a carafe of wine, he was spreading a quilt on the carpet in front of the fireplace. When he was done, he went around the room turning off lights until the only illumination was the moonlight from the windows and the firelight from the hearth.

She had set the tray on the coffee table and poured the wine. He picked up both glasses and extended one to her. Her fingers were trembling so that she could barely hold the fragile crystal. He clinked their glasses together and then sipped from his while he watched her over the rim.

"Will you do me a favor?" he asked quietly. He took her glass and returned it with his to the tray.

"A favor?"

"I have a trick muscle in my back that bothers me now and then. Today when I was starting the motor on the boat, I aggravated it."

"Tyler," she exclaimed softly. "Is it serious?"

"Nothing a good backrub won't cure." He reached for her hand and pulled her to him. "You can start by helping me out of my clothes."

She swallowed a lump of self-consciousness but kept her hand where he had placed it at the open collar of his shirt. Putting aside her last remnant of caution, she undid the buttons of his shirt. She pulled it out of the waistband of his trousers and pushed it off his shoulders. The shirt was negligently dropped onto the sofa. A mere piece of cloth couldn't compete with the sight of his chest for her attention. Her eyes took in each nuance of his rugged build.

"You may do the belt and pants in two separate steps, or combine the two. It's up to you."

She looked down at his belt with the simple buckle and sighed in relief. With her fingers shaking as they were, she didn't think she could have handled anything intricate. Unbuckling the belt didn't intimidate her, but unbuttoning the trousers was the most brazen thing she had ever had to bring herself to do. At least she thought so until she had to unzip them.

"I'd never hurt you, Hailey." The words came huskily from just above her head.

Her fingers found the zipper's tab and she pulled it down. Her heart was thudding and she feared for what would happen next. As usual, Tyler surprised her. He stepped back as he kicked off his loafers.

"Thank you," he said. His socks followed his shoes. Then he was stepping out of his trousers without a modicum of modesty. He tossed them across the back of a chair. The deep shadows in the room cast the angles of his body into sharp relief. He looked stronger, larger, more masculine than he had at the swimming pool. In truth she was seeing no more of him now than she had then. But there was a difference, if only psychological, between swimming trunks and a scrap of soft white cotton.

She jumped back a step when he went down on one knee in front of her. "Don't you want to get out of these boots?" He looked up at her, his eyes lit with the shine of firelight.

"Y . . . yes," she said. Leaning down, she propped her hands on his bare shoulders for balance. His hands caressed the backs of her calves as he eased the boots off one by one.

"There. That's bound to feel better," he said as he lay down on his stomach on the quilt and stretched luxuriously. "My life's in your hands, Hailey."

Feeling awkward and naive, she knelt beside him. Her shy hands were inches from his back when he spoke again, and she drew back skittishly. "Feel free to get more comfortable whenever you like."

"I'm fine," she said quickly.

He shrugged, a motion that set the muscles of his back into play. "There's no rush." He rested his cheek on his folded hands. "The bad muscle is just under my right shoulder blade. There's some lotion there by the sofa," he added, indicating the plastic bottle on the floor. His eyes closed.

Somewhere she had read that the proper way to give a massage was to put the lotion in the palm of one's hand rather than pour it directly onto the skin. That way it would be warm before application. She squeezed a dollop of the rich lotion into her palm and smoothed it between her hands. Taking a deep breath, she placed her hands on the tanned flesh of his shoulders.

Her motions were timid at first, but she soon gained confidence when he didn't move or protest her amateurish method. She worked her hands slowly over the broad expanse of his back, then concentrated on the spot that was bothering him. Her fingers gently kneaded. Her palms pressed.

"You're a born masseuse," he mumbled.

"Am I?" she asked, not knowing that her breath fanned the skin of his back.

"A magic touch."

"You mean I don't rub you the wrong way?" she asked teasingly.

He cocked a brow over a derisive eye as he twisted his head around to look at her. "You've got a whole new career ahead of you—the world's only *comédienne* masseuse."

"I'd go broke in no time."

"You could use some more practice." He shocked

her by rolling over onto his back. "If you go into the massaging business, you'll have to be fully educated. Better learn how to do the front, too."

Their eyes met and Hailey recognized the challenge. He was daring her. His chest rose and fell with his easy breathing. His flat stomach sloping down from his rib cage invited her to trace the silky growth of hair that disappeared beneath his underwear. One knee came up to a bent position, making his attitude one of relaxed confidence. It was a gauntlet that Hailey couldn't afford to ignore.

Never taking her eyes from his, she poured more lotion in her palm. Being deliberately slow and sensuous, she spread the emulsion between her hands, sliding the fingers of one hand through those of the other. Then she bent over him and placed a hand on either side of his neck. Working outward, she strolled across his shoulders and down his upper arms. She tilted her chin back arrogantly and watched him through half-closed eyes as she squeezed his hard muscles. Alternately contracting and releasing her fingers, she worked them down to the inside of his elbow. There her fingernails lightly raked his sensitized skin.

"You've just sealed your fate, Hailey," he growled. Reaching behind her, he cupped her head in one hand and forced it down to meet his scorching kiss. To brace herself, she put her hands on either side of his head on the quilt. He slanted his mouth across hers, kissing her with naked hunger. His tongue swept her mouth thoroughly, before employ-

ing finesse to bring her to a state of quivering
arousal.

Her elbows weakened and, unable to support herself
any longer, she slumped against him. His mouth followed the curve of her throat. He wasn't deterred by
her blouse, but kissed her through it, burying his face
between her breasts and enjoying the fullness with his
nose and chin.

He sat up, pushing her to a sitting position as he
did. His hand moved from the back of her head to rub
his thumb across her bottom lip. "Now it's your turn,"
he whispered. She was held spellbound by his hypnotic eyes as his fingers began working the buttons
down her back. When all were released, he eased her
blouse over her shoulders and down her arms.

"You're so pretty, Hailey," he said, trailing a finger along the curve of her breasts that the fragile lace
and nylon of a half-bra couldn't contain. He drew her
to her knees and unfastened her skirt. Without speaking, he indicated what he wanted her to do.

She stood and stepped out of her skirt with a feminine grace that made him smile. With one irrevocable
motion, she divested herself of half-slip and panty
hose. Then she was standing before him in panties and
bra. She wasn't brave enough to meet his eyes, but she
watched his hand as it came up to take hers.

"Lie down," he directed softly. She lay down on her
stomach as he had done, and pressed her fevered
cheek against her hands. Without actually watching,

she could follow his actions as he poured lotion in his hands, rubbed them together, then laid them on her.

Each stroke was calculated. His fingers were quick and light or slow and hard, but constantly changing tempo. Under his practiced touch, she concentrated on holding herself still when she wanted to squirm and writhe with increasing restlessness.

The brassiere strap across her back came away with one deft flick of his wrist. Her breath came unsteadily when his fingers drew a line from under her arms to her waist with agonizing, enticing leisure. With no objection from her, her panties went the way of the bra when his hands encountered the garment. Indeed, of their own will, her hips lifted to accommodate him.

All control vanished when she felt his hands on the backs of her thighs. Her breath quickened to rapid panting as he worked the creamy lotion into her skin. The backs of her knees, her calves, and the soles of her feet knew the strength and tenderness of his touch.

She ground her forehead against the quilt and stifled a moan of pure, animal pleasure when she felt his hair-roughened thighs closing around her hips as he straddled her. His hands slipped under her to fondle her breasts as he stretched above her. Instantly she knew that at some point he had rid himself of his underwear. He was a delicious weight to bear. She could feel the hair on his chest tickling the skin on her back.

Placing his mouth against her ear, he said with unbridled urgency, "Hailey, let me love you. Now, my love, before I die of wanting you."

He levered himself above her until she turned to lie facing him. His eyes ran the length of her. Everywhere they touched, her skin felt like it had been prickled with the sparks that fly from a sparkler. Then, slowly, as one humbly accepts a long awaited tribute, he lowered his body over hers.

He kissed her. The kiss was exquisitely sweet. His tongue barely penetrated her lips, outlined the shape of them, investigated the inside of them, rubbed against her tongue. Greedy now that all the shackles had been loosened, her own tongue darted past his lips.

Her kiss unleashed his driving passion. Randomly, his mouth ran over her, partaking of her flesh like a man starved. Her breasts knew the blissful torment of his lips, her nipples the gentle lashing of his tongue. He kissed his way over the flat plain of her stomach to her navel, where he used the erotic powers of his mouth to full advantage. Her fingers burrowed in his hair and she cried his name when his kisses burned along the tender flesh inside her thighs.

"Hailey." He said her name with the reverence of a prayer as he covered her again. She welcomed him, moving as he guided her with the adjustments of his own body. Kissing her deeply, he probed her tentatively and met only pliant acceptance. "Hailey, sweet Hailey," he murmured as he claimed her in the timeless and most eternal of ways.

She knew only a flash of pain and fear when he breached the last barrier of her innocence. Then she was caught up in the wonder of it all as wave after wave of incredible feeling washed over her. "Tyler." She hadn't even realized that she had said his name until he stilled and lifted his head to look down into her radiant face.

"Am I hurting you, Hailey? Tell me and—"

"No," she said, capturing his face between her palms and lowering it to kiss him. "No, no. I never knew . . . I never imagined . . ." She arched her throat as another sensation seized her and lifted her hips to know more of him.

"Take all of me, Hailey," he groaned as he laid his head next to hers. "That's it. Yes, my love, move with me. That's it. Oh, God, so perfect."

The universe could have been extinguished for all she knew, for all she cared. The revelation that burst upon her brain was like a blinding light that could have replaced the sun. This had been ordained, prescribed by Fate, predestined. And as thrilling as it was, it wasn't the act itself from which she derived this transporting ecstasy, but from the man. Never would she share this with another.

She loved Tyler Scott.

Their movements were perfectly matched, a blending of spirits as well as bodies. She surrendered her love, her life, to him. He filled her, expanding her soul until they exploded in a simultaneous celebration of life.

For long moments, they lay still, locked in that most intimate of embraces. Her face turned into his and they breathed each other's breath. When the pounding of his heart, which she felt inside her own breasts, had calmed, he kissed her brow.

"It is not you who has been seduced, my love. But I."

CHAPTER 10

"Are you trying to get me drunk?" she asked as he pushed another glass of cold, white wine on her.

"Naturally. Isn't that what debauchers of virgins do? Get them drunk and then get them naked?"

"I'm already naked."

He grinned and raked her with lascivious eyes. "So you are," he drawled. Leaning forward from his sitting position, he buried his face in the hair that rioted around her head in enchanting disarray. "And I'm already drunk. On you."

The kiss was long and deep and some of the wine was spilled onto the carpet. When at last Hailey pulled away, she sighed contentedly. He chuckled softly. "Does it feel that good?"

Her eyes were misty and slumberous, a green watercolor in her flushed face. "Yes," she whispered convincingly. "It feels that good."

His hand came up to marvel over the softness of her cheek. "To me, too, Hailey." Carrying her with him, he fell back against the pillows they had taken from the couch and piled on the quilt before the fire. She stretched along his length, propping herself on her elbows and leaning over him as he caressed her arms and shoulders.

"I was afraid that I'd be . . . well, awkward . . . not good for . . ."

He stilled her lips by placing an imperative index finger over them. "You were perfect." He searched her troubled eyes for a long moment then said softly, "Acceptance is crucial to you, isn't it, Hailey. Why? You do everything well. You're beautiful."

"I wasn't until I met you," she said with tender gratitude.

His finger followed the hairline across her forehead. "You've always been, you just didn't know it. What fool made you feel you weren't beautiful? A man?"

"No," she answered slowly, self-consciously. "Not one particular man, that is. I've never felt—"

"You're saying the human race in general made you feel unattractive? I don't buy that, Hailey. Sure, you must have had some years during adolescence when you weren't a raving beauty. But do any of us look our best during that time? No, you had that complex germinating inside you long before then."

"I suppose so," she said, privately viewing her childhood. "I never was fawned over, petted, the way Ellen was. I was the elder. It was up to me to set a good example. When Ellen fell out of favor, her transgression was quickly forgiven because she didn't take punishment well. She would carry on until Mother and

Daddy were miserable over whatever meager punishment they had doled out. I took punishment stoically, never letting them know how bad I felt. Perhaps that was my mistake.

"And then, Ellen truly was an adorable child. Naughtiness only made her more appealing. I was merely good. I guess the adage 'The squeaky wheel gets the oil' applied to the way our parents treated us. I never caused any trouble, so I was easy to ignore."

"Who could ignore you?" he asked. His eyes dropped to her breasts which rose and fell so alluringly close to his eyes. "Especially men."

Hailey laughed. "When you're three inches taller than most of the boys in high school, you're generally ignored. As a sex symbol, at any rate. While I was in college, I was taking care of my parents, too, and that curbed my social life considerably. And by the time I graduated and went to work—"

"You had built up a wall of insecurities as a defense against the slings and arrows, so to speak. You wouldn't let any romantically inclined gentleman close enough to penetrate it."

Her smile was gaminelike when she looked down at him through lowered lashes and said demurely, *"You* penetrated it."

He laughed with pure delight, then lowered his voice to a seductive rumble. "I love it when you talk dirty." She laughed with him, tossing her hair back over her shoulders in a careless gesture that she didn't even know was sexy.

The laughter subsided and she shyly averted her eyes. "Tyler, teach . . . teach me to . . . I want to please you."

He looked up at her and thought that she couldn't please him any more than she did already. Her hair, the eyes that revealed so much, the glow of her skin polished with the golden light of the fire, combined to create a picture of female loveliness that made him wish he could paint, or write poetry, so she would be preserved for future generations to enjoy.

But he would be consumed by jealousy if he had to share her with anyone. After tonight he would be tempted to lock her away from the rest of the world. He had always been greedy, selfish, proud of his possessions, his accumulated wealth. Yet he would give away anything he owned in exchange for her. Her soul, her mind, her body.

Her lips were swollen and moist from his loving. He knew their provocative talents. When he had first kissed her, he had met maidenly resistance. Now, her mouth opened to him freely, giving, receiving. But out of that same mouth came clever witticisms and educated insights. She stimulated his intellect as much and as often as she stimulated his body. He was constantly challenged by her keen mind. But that wasn't what she wanted to hear now. She sought another kind of reassurance.

How could she be so unaware that she lacked nothing in sexuality? He was already aroused merely by the sight of her. Her breasts were ripe for loving. The dark apricot nipples were delicate. He wanted to feel them between his lips, under the coaxing of his tongue. *Hailey, don't you know, don't you see your own prowess?*

"This will be the shortest lesson in your life," he said. "You already have pleased me."

"I want to learn more."

He drew her down to him and covered her mouth with his. Her hair fell on either side of his face, a fragrant curtain that he wished could cloak all of him. As though he were taking small, savoring bites out of a juicy peach, his lips opened and closed over hers. His tongue systematically investigated the interior of her mouth, surveying it, cataloging each texture, memorizing each mystery.

He drew back and waited and then congratulated himself on the excellent teacher he was. Hailey practiced her new skills but brought to them an application uniquely her own. Tyler shuddered with the agony of restraint.

His lips ravaged her ears, her throat, and she mimicked him, but surpassed him in talent. She wielded her dainty tongue like a weapon until he choked her name and hugged her to him, stilling her, until he could once again exercise control.

Her breasts filled his hands and he rubbed the lush mounds until he felt the centers swelling in his palms. Then his fingers circled them slowly until they were hard, throbbing buds of desire. He soothed them with his tongue.

Hailey looked at him in wonder when he lowered

his head onto the pillows. His fingers continued to stroke and brush. "That, too?" she asked.

"Yes."

She looked at his impressive chest and tentatively fanned her fingers over the crinkly hair. "I like the way you look, Tyler."

"It's mutual . . . ah, Hailey . . ."

Her nails lightly raked his nipple and it grew hard. Then she kissed her way across his chest until her lips found it.

"Yes, yes," he moaned when her tongue dared to push past her lips to taste him.

Without waiting for further instruction, motivated only by the evident pleasure she brought to him, loving him, she kissed her way down that intriguing arrow of hair on his stomach. His hands lost themselves in the violent mass of her hair and he repeated her name like a chant as she kissed each rib in turn.

His hands left her breasts. One went around her to cup her hips, the other found that dark auburn delta at the top of her thighs. His hand flattened over her, applying a rotating pressure she felt as much from the inside as without. Searching with tenderness, he loved her with his fingertips.

"Please, Hailey, please."

She knew what he wanted of her. Love made the unthinkable possible. She touched his body reverently. The miracle of him wasn't lost on her and she gloried in it. Wanting to feel that life force bursting inside her

SEDUCTION BY DESIGN   181

again, she rolled to her back and guided him to the
threshold of all her desire.

"Hailey, no," he said with concern, even as she
thrust herself against him.

"Yes, yes."

No longer the teacher, Tyler learned from her. He
tried to keep a rein on his desire, but her demands
wouldn't let him. In a final helpless surge of passion,
he took them both to a final shattering fulfillment.

Self-disgust was written on his face when he left her
and collapsed onto his back beside her. "I'm sorry,
Hailey. I knew I was hurting you. I didn't mean to
make love to you again so soon. I wouldn't hurt you
for anything in the world. Will you forgive me?"

She laid her head on his beating heart and closed her
arms around him. "I would never have forgiven you if
you hadn't."

"You look kinda cute like that," she teased as she
stepped out of the shower. Tyler was at the basin, his
hips wrapped in a towel, the lower half of his face lathered with shaving cream.

"You don't look bad yourself," he said, eyeing her
in the mirror. She curtsied impishly. "If you'll stop acting like a brat, I'll tell you that that shower was the
most erotic experience I've ever had. It outdid even
my wildest fantasies. I honestly don't know how we
kept from drowning."

He chuckled as the razor took one long stroke from
the base of his throat up to his jaw. "I see you can still

blush. Despite all your wanton ways, Miss Ashton, you are still a prude."

"You think so?" she taunted, coming up behind him and wrapping her arms around his waist. He accommodated her by settling himself back against her. "What can I do to show you that I have absolutely no scruples left?" The tips of her breasts tantalized his back.

The razor was poised over his Adam's apple, but judiciously he didn't touch it to his skin. "I'm sure you'll think of something."

With a sudden movement, she yanked the towel from around his waist and threw it to the floor.

"You're right," he said gruffly as she pressed herself against him, "you couldn't get more shameless than that."

The wandering fingers that slipped below his waist proved him wrong. His breath hissed through clenched teeth. The razor was dropped into the basin. He whirled around and, taking her off guard, bent down to grab her under the hips and raise her off the floor. Forgetting the frosting of shaving cream on his face, he buried it between her breasts, still dewy and warm from the shower.

"At this rate I'll die young but sated," he mumbled. His mouth traveled from the bewitching valley to the tempting crests, planting firm kisses everywhere it touched.

Hailey twisted away from him and cried out. He knew the way she spoke to him in passion and he knew instantly that this was different. He jerked his head back to look at her worriedly.

"Tyler," she gasped, tears forming in her eyes. "That shaving cream, is it *mentholated*?"

"I'll pay you back," she warned, dripping raw egg from the wire whisk she shook at him. Joining her in the kitchen where she was preparing a hearty breakfast, he had made the mistake of asking her—with a broad grin splitting his handsome face—how she felt. "You couldn't even help me wash it off you were laughing so hard."

"I'm sorry, Hailey," he said contritely, though he couldn't disguise the mischievous lights dancing in his eyes. "I didn't think. Honest. Scout's honor."

She scoffed at his penitent expression. "Humility doesn't fit you at all. You were born to be arrogant, overbearing, and conceited. But you're forgiven if you'll set the table."

"Okay, but first things first." He came to her and encircled her with possessive arms. Finding her mouth unerringly, he kissed her with a hunger that hadn't been satisfied even through the long hours of the night.

When they had at last left the quilt in front of the fireplace for his king-size bed, they promised each other they would sleep. It was a worthless pledge that neither could keep. His suggestion that they practice caution—in deference to her recently lost virginity— fell on deaf ears.

Now they caressed and kissed with renewed vigor.

Each embrace only enhanced their desire. The butter sizzling in the skillet until it burned and filled the kitchen with acrid smoke brought them to their senses. They didn't even mind cleaning the skillet and starting over again.

Hailey was feeding him a last scrap of bacon off her own plate when he said, "I need to call Atlanta and check on some things. Do you think you can manage to amuse yourself until I get done?" He licked her fingers free of bacon grease, then decided they weren't quite clean and started the procedure again.

She watched as each finger was drawn between his lips with a gentle suction. His teeth raked against her fingertips. The words she framed in her mind had a hard time finding their way to her mouth. "I . . . uh . . . I guess I can clean up the kitchen."

"Call me if you need me," he breathed as he kissed her once again.

Twenty minutes later she found him in his bedroom sitting on the side of the bed, listening in deep concentration to whomever was speaking on the other end of the line. "Okay, but someone messed up. Find out where the breakdown was by this time tomorrow. I'll want to know then how you intend to get back in the customer's favor." He slammed the receiver down without another word, and Hailey felt pity for the employee who had come under such criticism.

"Troubles?" she asked softly and touched his hair.

"Yes," he grumbled absently. Then as if realizing for the first time that she was there, he pulled her down onto his lap. "To hell with all that," he said, stretching her sweater tight across her breasts and looking at the results with evident pleasure.

"When do you have to get back?"

"I don't know," he said distractedly, still absorbed in his project to display her breasts to their best advantage. He looked at her then and grinned. "But if we stay much longer, I'm going to have to go out and buy more vitamins. A man my age can't keep up this sexual marathon without reinforcements."

"Yes," she sighed theatrically. "You're really quite old. Gray hair," she said, threading her fingers through the silver at his temples, "waning strength, no stamina."

He took her hand and squeezed it tight "Hailey, there's something I should have told you before."

His tone was so clipped and his face so serious that her heart lurched with dread. He had four illegitimate children? He wasn't as rich as he pretended? He owed the Mafia money? *What?* Whatever it was, she'd stand by him. She could face anything with him. Only, please God, don't let it be his health. Anything but that. *Please.* Her fingers were still lovingly sifting through his hair "What, Tyler?" she asked solicitously.

"You have a hell of a cute fanny."

She shoved him backward as she shot off his lap. Pulling one of the pillows from under the spread, she pounded him with it while he covered his head with protective arms. "I really had you going there, didn't I, Red? But I only told you the truth."

"Well I can't wait to show it off to all the boys in the neighborhood," she said as she dropped the pillow on his head and spun on her heels.

"Where are you going?"

"To fetch your daughter," she called over her shoulder, swaying the object of his admiration saucily in her tight jeans. "And we may never come back."

"Yes, you will. You crave my body too much," he shouted after her.

She was still laughing when she slammed the front door behind her. The whole world was suddenly right. Her footsteps were light as she walked up the gravel lane toward the Harpers' house, which she and Tyler had located last night after leaving the restaurant. Strange that last night she had dreaded what the Harpers would think of her when Faith told them that she wasn't Mrs. Scott. Now she didn't care at all.

What she had given to Tyler had been given out of love. No one could take the splendor away from her. She wasn't naive enough to think that it would last forever. She hadn't been the first woman in Tyler's life and she wouldn't be the last. But while she was with him, she was going to squeeze the last ounce of pleasure from it. This was a once-in-a-lifetime affair. He was the only man she would ever love. Of that she was certain.

She had walked the half-mile or so to the Harpers' house in no time. Mrs. Harper greeted her warmly rather than with the righteous indignation Hailey had expected.

"Faith is an absolute delight. She and Kim exchanged addresses, so each would know when the other was going to be here. We live in Asheville but we come up here often on the weekends. I hope they can get together again."

"I hope so, too. Thank you for inviting her."

Kim and Faith said an emotional good-bye with promises to write. Faith's depression was soon forgotten as they walked back toward the house. She was bubbling over with things to tell Hailey.

"Her mom was s-o-o-o-o nice. She gave Kim a bunch of makeup she didn't use anymore and we tried it all! Only we had to promise to wash it off before we went to bed. And we played Atari, but not too long. Mostly we listened to records and talked. It was s-o-o-o-o neat."

"But did you have a good time?" Hailey asked ironically. It took Faith a moment to catch the teasing in Hailey's voice, but then they hugged each other and laughed.

"Yes, but I missed you and Daddy."

Hailey was struck by how easily the words went together. You and Daddy. A unit. "Did you?" she asked. Emotion made the words sound gravelly.

"Yes. Kim's mom and dad were nice, but they're not as neat as you and Daddy are. Her mom's not near as pretty as you."

"Thank you, but you really shouldn't judge someone by how he looks, you know."

"I know, but I couldn't help noticing."

Hailey was tempted to ask what Faith had said about her—if the Harpers knew she and Tyler weren't married—but she couldn't quite bring herself to.

"I wonder who that is," Faith said, bringing Hailey's attention to the car parked in the circle driveway in front of the house.

Hailey faltered and her heart sank with disappointment. Ellen. How had she located them? What could she possibly want?

"It's my sister's car." She released Faith's hand and opened the front door. Faith went in first, but just inside the door she stopped abruptly. A fraction of a second later, Hailey, too, was struck motionless.

Ellen and Tyler were standing in front of the fireplace, which was cold and gray now with ash. Ellen's arms were locked behind his head. The heels of his hands were at her ribs. Their bodies were plastered together from chest to knee as they kissed.

Having heard the intruders, he shoved Ellen away from him. She blinked up at him stupidly until she followed the direction of his surprised, guilty gaze. His eyes locked with Hailey's, and in them she saw a chasm of regret and remorse opening up, widening, threatening to swallow her.

"Hi, Hailey," Ellen chirped.

"Shut up!" Tyler barked. "Hailey—"

"Go to hell," she said calmly. She turned away from

them and made for her bedroom, where she planned to gather her things together and leave before she was sickened and humiliated further.

"Hailey, stop," Tyler ordered. When she didn't obey, but hurried her suddenly leaden feet, he bounded after her. He caught her at the doorway and grabbed her shoulders from behind.

"Let me go," she screamed, twisting away from the iron strength of his hands.

"No. I know what you're thinking and you're wrong. Think about it and you'll know how wrong you are."

"You couldn't possibly know what I'm thinking," she spat.

"Like hell I don't. I know that proud thrust of your chin, that ramrod spine. It means you've made up your mind about something and nothing can change it. But, by God, you're going to listen to me while I explain what you saw."

"What I saw was self-explanatory."

A blistering expletive was pushed through his teeth, but he didn't release her. He kept her pinned against the wall. She raised murderous green eyes to him. Later she would die of the hurt. Now all she felt was a blinding rage.

"You got what you wanted last night. Your seduction was carried out. So now you've gone on to another challenge. Isn't that what your life consists of? Challenges? Gambles? Well, congratulations. You won the game with me. Now let go."

For a moment his eyes lost their anger, and in them she saw pain. "Do you think no more of me than that Hailey?" It was a harsh, low whisper that only she could hear, but she was stricken by the disillusionment it conveyed.

Then his eyes went as hard as flint again. "Ellen," he shouted.

"What?" Ellen said sulkily from the position she had maintained by the fireplace.

"Come here."

"What—"

"Dammit, I said to come here," Tyler roared. Ellen didn't dare disobey that fearsome command. When she was a few steps away, he anchored Hailey against the wall with a steel forearm across her collarbone and reached behind him to drag Ellen up to them. "Tell her why you came here."

Ellen looked first at Tyler with her wide, green eyes, then at Hailey. After licking her lips, she said, "I came here to ask him for a loan."

Hailey sagged under Tyler's ruthless hold, but he didn't relax it. For a moment she forgot him and the unscaleable wall between them, and looked with dismay at her sister. "You *what*?"

Ellen's lower lip began to tremble. "They fired me from my job, Hailey. Just because I took a few days off last week because I wasn't feeling well. When I went to work yesterday morning, they told me to clean out my desk. They were so mean to me." She was sobbing in earnest now.

"But why did you come to Tyler, asking for money?"

Ellen sniffed prettily and her tears clung to her lashes like dewdrops. "I went to you first. I went to Serendipity and they told me you and Tyler had come here. So I followed."

"I gave you money last week, Ellen. Surely you've got severance pay coming."

She darted another fearful look at Tyler before turning back to Hailey. "I didn't pay my rent last month. I had so many other things I had to buy. So now my landlord is threatening to evict me. They're not paying me severance because I took a few sick days. And even if I find another job right away, it'll be weeks before I get a check.

"He's got a lot of money, Hailey," she said referring to Tyler. "I knew he could loan me some and not even miss it. When I found out you were with him, I decided it was a better idea to ask him instead of you."

"Oh, my God." Hailey closed her eyes and bowed her head in shame that her own flesh and blood could be so unconscionable.

"Tell her about the kiss." Tyler's voice was low, deep, but intimidating.

"He . . . he said we could work something out—"

He jerked on Ellen's arm roughly and Hailey wondered how it managed to remain in its socket. Ellen's eyes went wide with fear and her face paled significantly.

"Tell her the truth!"

"Hailey, I . . . You wouldn't mind . . . You'd know I was only teasing . . ."

"When her tearful pleas didn't work, she tried another tack. She flung her arms around my neck and started kissing me. That's when you walked in." Tyler's eyes had been riveted on Hailey's as he told her what had happened. Now he swung his head to Ellen and released her arm so quickly he could have been shaking her off like some hideous insect. "Get out." The words fell into the room like stones.

"Get out?" Ellen asked, aghast. "You can't—"

"I damn well can. Get out."

"Hailey," Ellen said, ignoring him. "You've got to help me." Her voice was a wheedling whine.

"Why should she?" Tyler asked. "Because she always has before? Those days are over, Ellen. Get back to Nashville and wait to hear from me. I think you'd fit in very nicely in a small company I have in Baltimore."

"Baltimore! But that's—"

"Too far for you to come running to Hailey for a handout. Now get out of here before I give you the beating you've deserved all your life."

"Are you going to let him do this to me?" Ellen demanded of Hailey.

Hailey raised her head. It had seemed like too much of an effort to hold it erect. Never had she felt so defeated. "I don't care what you do, Ellen. Just leave me alone."

Ellen's face crumpled like that of a child who is

about to cry. "Oh, you always were so mean! You never did anything wrong! Perfect, little goody-two-shoes Hailey. Well, nobody liked you and everybody loved me." She ran to the door and flung it open. "Even he likes me better than he does you. He just doesn't want to admit it, but he *was* kissing me back!" The door slammed behind her. Seconds later they heard the motor of her car being raced to life. Then silence.

The room was perfectly still. Hailey could hear Tyler's watch ticking near her ear as he kept her backed to the wall. He could have saved his effort. The fight had long since gone out of her. All that was left of her was an empty shell. Had he not been holding her up, she might well have folded into a heap on the floor. The day that had started in such a haze of happiness had now gone black with despair.

"She's lying, Hailey."

"It doesn't matter."

"It matters," he said, shaking her slightly.

She shook her head. "No. This has been wrong from the beginning. I knew what you wanted of me. You got it. The rest was just playacting for all of us. It was wrong for you, for me, for Faith—"

She broke off suddenly, realizing the terrible scene the child had witnessed. Peering around Tyler's shoulders, her eyes swept the room, looking for the girl. "Faith?" she asked softly. Her eyes rose to Tyler's.

He let go of her and turned around, making the same cursory inspection of the room she had. Without having to communicate their thoughts, they separated. Hailey checked the kitchen and the back part of the house. Tyler looked in all the bedrooms and ran around the outside perimeter of the house, scanning the lakeshore as he did so.

They met back in the living room, each asking with apprehensive, hopeful eyes, each getting a negative answer from the other.

Tyler seemed truly bewildered and lost when he said, "She's gone."

CHAPTER | 11

Hailey's fingers mashed against her compressed lips. "Oh, Tyler, she must have been terribly distressed by what she heard."

"Yes, she would have been," he said, raking his fingers through his hair. "Monica and I were barely civil whenever we had to meet. Faith was frequently subjected to shouting scenes. I swore to myself that she'd never know that kind of confusion and fear again. Dammit! It's a good thing that bitch left or I might very well have killed her."

"It wasn't entirely Ellen's fault."

"Don't you dare start defending her," he flared, his eyes flashing menacingly. "We both just did her the biggest favor of her life. She'll land on her feet. Her type usually does—after having walked all over your type."

Hailey looked away, knowing he was right. Ellen had reacted like the spoiled child she would always be, but she would come back with professions of love when she needed Hailey again. Dismissing her sister from her mind, Hailey focused on the more immediate problem of Faith. "Where do you think she would go?"

"I don't know," Tyler said in agitation. "I've got to find her and talk to her. She's probably not in a very sound emotional state."

"She couldn't have gone far. We'll find her soon."

They couldn't have known how wrong that prediction would prove to be. They agreed that Tyler would search the woods behind the house, while Hailey called the Harpers and then looked along the lakeshore. When those expeditions proved fruitless, they got in the car and searched the backroads and the wooded areas lining them. No one at the lodge had seen Faith that morning and the man managing the electronic games area assured them that he had been there since opening and would have seen her had she come in.

"What does she look like?" he asked them again. "I'll check around."

"She's eleven years old. Has brown pigtails and eyes the color of mine," Tyler said. "Tall, thin, braces on her teeth."

"What was she wearing?"

"Hell, man, I don't—"

"She was wearing jeans and a blue-and-red-striped sweater," Hailey interceded quickly.

Their search stretched into hours. With each passing minute, Tyler's composure dwindled. Fighting her own growing panic, Hailey tried to reason with him, but he only grew more impatient with her banal assurances, recognizing them for what they were. He blamed himself for Faith's disappearance. Hailey's own feeling of guilt was just as strong. And though neither pointed an accusing finger at the other, they couldn't quite meet each other's eyes.

When by mid-afternoon Faith still hadn't been found, they called in the local police force, which began combing the foothills and lakeshore in a full-fledged search. Hailey heard one patrolman mention something about dragging the lake to another, and her blood ran cold. Luckily, Tyler had been giving a thorough description of Faith to another officer and hadn't heard that grim possibility.

As the daylight faded, his belligerence increased. The patrolmen ignored his verbal abuse, knowing that it stemmed from the mind of a frantic parent. Hailey wanted to comfort him, but she couldn't. She had no platitudes to offer, for the possibilities of what could have happened to Faith were limitless and terrifying. She was having a hard time keeping herself from giving way to hysteria.

Long after dusk, they were still awaiting word from the many who were out looking for the girl. The chief officer had commissioned Tyler and Hailey to stay in the house, should he need to call, or should Faith show up there.

For the thousandth time, Hailey's eyes swept over the living room as she nervously dallied with one of her earrings. The silence was almost tangible. The telephone remained mute. The atmosphere was like that of a wake. No, worse, Hailey thought. It was like waiting for a surgeon's report on a life-or-death operation. Not knowing was the worst part.

Tyler sat on the sofa, staring at the floor between his widespread knees. His head was bowed low. His hair was mussed. The lines around his eyes and mouth were deeply etched with worry. Mud and leaves clung to his casual shoes, reminders of his stubborn trekking through the woods behind the policemen.

It was heartrending to see a man of Tyler's arrogance reduced to such a level of humility and abject defeat. All day she had resisted going to him, touching him, embracing him. His suffering touched her deeply because she loved him so completely.

When had it happened? Last night when he had claimed her body and she had given it so freely? When she decided to come with him on this mini-vacation? No, long before that. When? Or had it always been there, waiting for her to admit it? She didn't remember consciously choosing to love him, she only knew that she did and probably always had, right from the moment he'd first spoken to her.

Is this who we've been waiting an eternity for?

Had she fallen in love with him even then, when his slate gray eyes had bored into hers with frustration and . . . what? What had she seen that day in Tyler's face that had changed her forever?

Whatever had made her love him, whenever it had happened, it was there now, consuming her, filling her with such joy that she wanted to shout about it. Perhaps she did, for at that moment his head snapped up to look at her. She was appalled at the ravaged look on his face. The silent appeal in his red-rimmed eyes pulled at her heartstrings.

"Hailey . . . ?"

The appeal was silent no longer. She heard it. And she knew what it had cost a man of Tyler's arrogance to make it. By speaking no more than her name, he had uttered a plea for her help.

Without hesitation she rose from her chair and rushed across the space that separated them to fling her arms around him.

"Tyler, Tyler," she whispered as his head was buried between her breasts. It wasn't a passionate action, but one of desperation. An infant seeking solace, a human being needing the touch of another. His arms closed around her with unabashed need.

Tightly, she clutched him to her, stroking the tension out of his shoulders with loving hands. She bent her head over his and kissed his temples, his eyebrows, his silver hair. Whatever she had to give belonged to him.

Because she loved him so fiercely, she was giving him license to hurt and misuse her more than anyone else ever had, yet it didn't matter. He needed her. It was within her power to help him. To deny him herself was unthinkable. Just as she had given him her body last night, she now gave him her soul and spirit without qualification.

"Tyler," she said, laying her cheek on top of his head. "Tyler, I love you."

She held her breath. For a long moment neither of them moved. Had he heard her? Was he shocked? Revolted? Thrilled? He raised his head slowly. Then, when she didn't think she could stand the suspense any longer, she looked into those gray eyes that cut through her like a rapier.

Before either of them could speak, the back door opened quietly. The metal latch clicked shut. Tyler's head jerked toward the sound as though to confirm he hadn't been dreaming. Hailey came off the sofa, her hands clenched at her waist as she took two hesitant steps toward the kitchen.

Faith appeared in the doorway that connected the two rooms. She was dirty. Tears had left two muddy tracks down her cheeks. The knees of her jeans were filthy and threadbare. Leaves and twigs littered her hair. It wasn't her appearance, however, that stunned them. It was the hateful glare in her eyes.

"Faith," Tyler said. His shoulders slumped in relief. "Where have you been?"

"In the woods."

"All this time? Didn't you hear us calling you?"

"Yes. But I didn't answer. I didn't want you to find me. I didn't want to come back here to you. I wanted to die."

Her words were spoken with such venom that Tyler's hasty footsteps toward her were checked. He stared at his daughter uncomprehendingly. He seemed at a complete loss. His arms hung loosely at his sides. Wanting to rush to his child and hug her tight to reassure himself that she was really home safe, he was stunned by her antipathy. He turned back toward Hailey for help. She met his baffled eyes with the same sense of puzzlement.

"We've been very worried about you, Faith," she said to the girl. "Your father was sick with worry. We thought something terrible had happened to you."

"You wouldn't care!" she shouted. "No one would have cared if I'd died. No one likes me. My mother didn't. She was always telling me how stupid and ugly I am. She wanted to be with her friends all the time, never with me."

She rounded on her father. "You didn't want me to come live with you, either. You hate me, too. All you think about is work and making telephone calls and going off to meetings. You wish you didn't have me."

She was sobbing now, her small chest heaving with the emotions that ripped through her. Hailey's heart went out to her, but she didn't have a chance to soothe her before Faith turned to Hailey with unleashed wrath.

"You pretended to like me, but you don't. I was hoping that maybe you could live with us, be my mother, but you don't treat my daddy nice. If you'd hug and kiss him instead of always being stiff and shaky and mad when he touches you, then maybe he'd ask you to live with us. Last night I pretended with the Harpers that you were my mom. They kept telling me how

pretty my mom was. I wanted you to be my mom so
bad."

Convulsive sobs caused her to tremble convul-
sively. "But now I don't because you're *not* beautiful.
I think you're ugly. If you were beautiful and nice to
my daddy then he wouldn't have been kissing that
other ol' girl. I hate you." She glowered at Tyler. "I
hate you, too. I hate everybody." On that last wail she
ran to her room and slammed the door behind her.

Tyler didn't even wait a full second before he went
after her. Hailey ran to him, grabbing his arm. "No,
Tyler, let her cry it out for a while."

"Un-uh. She's not going to talk to you and me like
that and get away with it. Nor is she going to get by
with my nearly going insane with worry. It's time she
learned that she has some responsibilities in this world.
For running off and hiding all day, she deserves to be
punished."

Hailey's lips were rubbery, but she forced the words
out. "What are you going to do?"

"I'm going to spank her."

"No," she cried insistently, pulling on his arm. "No,
Tyler. She's upset—"

"So am I."

"But you're an adult. She's been put through a trau-
matic experience. Please. Wait a while. She doesn't understand—"

"Then it's time she did." He shook his arm free.

Hailey waited until she heard the door of Faith's
bedroom close behind him, then she ran out the front

door. The night air was cool as she ran down to the lakeshore, but she didn't notice it. The water was still, but no moon was reflected on its calm surface tonight. Clouds obliterated it. The magic had been for one night only.

How could everything have gone so wrong in such a short span of time? Or had she been deluding herself? Had it always been wrong for her to love Tyler? She had fallen in love with the man and had come to love the daughter. Now these two people whom she loved most in the world were suffering because of her interference in their life.

She had accused Tyler of using Faith to get close to her. But hadn't she done the same thing? Hadn't she used Faith to get to her father? She had been so subtle that she hadn't even realized what she had done until Faith's tirade against all the injustices in her young life pointed it out.

Realizing the disastrous effect of her presence in their lives, Hailey sank down on the pebbly shore and pressed her forehead against her raised knees. Unwittingly, she had driven a wedge into the tenuous relationship Tyler was carefully constructing with his daughter. Faith blamed her father for not marrying Hailey when the thought had probably never entered his mind. Faith blamed Hailey for not being good enough for him. Everyone lost.

During the long, passion-laden hours of the night before, Tyler had whispered love words in her ear. They had been poetically tender and shockingly bold.

They had stirred her to ecstasy and lulled her to sleep. But he had never said, "I love you," plainly and simply. His reaction to her speaking the words would forever remain a mystery, for she intended to leave first thing in the morning. She couldn't pursue a love affair with Tyler when Faith's happiness was at stake. Tyler couldn't either.

Hauling herself to her feet, she trudged back to the house. The door to Faith's bedroom was still closed, but she could hear faint murmurs of conversation. Going into her bedroom, she closed the door behind her. She was surrounded by a cold, dark loneliness. It was no stranger to her. She had lived with it for years. Only it was more noticeable now that she had had a glimpse of the other side.

Lethargically she prepared for bed, her mind and body exhausted. Knowing she should stay up and think about what she would do about her job at Serendipity—could she continue working for Tyler?—what she should do about Ellen, what she should do with the rest of her life without Tyler Scott in it, she couldn't resist collapsing onto the soft linens. She tried to tackle the problems tumbling through her brain, but her mind refused to cooperate. Within a few minutes after her head touched the pillow, she was asleep.

The first thing she saw when she sleepily opened her eyes the following morning was a denim-clad knee inches from the edge of the mattress. Following the length of sinewy thigh to its apex, she confirmed her lazy observation that the possessor of the knee was male. The sheer masculinity . . .

She sat bolt upright in bed, clutching the sheet against her "Serendipity sizzles!" T-shirt. "What are you doing in here?" she demanded.

"Sitting in a chair watching you sleep," Tyler said. His posture was little more than a slouch. He looked as disheveled as Hailey felt. His eyes were brooding under the broad slash of dark brow across his forehead.

"That's not funny," she said.

"It wasn't meant to be. You asked me what I was doing in here and I told you."

"How did you get in this room? I locked the door last night."

"I picked the lock."

Hailey cleared her throat and asked, "Faith? How is she?"

"She's fine," Tyler said, smiling for the first time. "In fact, she's a terrific person."

Hailey felt tears pricking her eyelids, thankful that their relationship hadn't been jeopardized by her bungling. "Did you spank her?"

"Yes," he answered slowly. "I also made her call the police and apologize to them for causing such a ruckus. And then we talked. She told me that she wished I had been around to spank her a long time ago." He laughed ruefully. "She didn't know I loved her, Hailey. I can't understand that, but she swears she didn't.

"From the viewpoint of a child whose mother was

more interested in her social calendar, whose father was absorbed in his business, who has never been on a picnic, I guess I *can* see how she might think she was not loved. Time and again I assured her she was and that I intend never to let her forget it. She won't be perfect from now on, but I think we reached the crisis point last night."

Nodding her head, Hailey smiled. He continued to stare at her, making her nervously aware of his dominating presence in the room. She gnawed her bottom lip and looked away from him. "What do you want?"

He ignored the question and asked one of his own. "Did you mean what you said last night just before Faith came in?"

For a fleeting instant she allowed her eyes to lock with his, then she concentrated on the ribbon-edged blanket as she said offhandedly, "It doesn't matter anymore."

He came out of the chair with a lunge to grab her by the shoulders. His knee dug a giant crater in the mattress. Grabbing a fistful of hair, he pulled her head back and leaned over her. Hailey stared up at him in fearful fascination.

"You have the most annoying habit of saying something doesn't matter when it matters a helluva lot." She had come under that same intimidating force of will earlier in the infirmary when he had wanted to know what happened to Faith. His whole countenance demanded an answer when he repeated, "Did you mean what you said?"

"Yes."

His mouth came down on hers, insistent and provocative. He parted her lips with a probing tongue. It swept her mouth with an ardency that left her breathless. When he raised his head, she fell back against the pillows, taking in great gulps of air.

One arm bridged her stomach as he leaned over her. "When we came out of her bedroom last night, Faith couldn't wait to apologize to you. She wanted you to know that she hadn't meant anything she'd said. We found you asleep and decided you needed that more than explanations. Later today she intends to tell you just how much you mean to her."

Hailey shook her head, staring unseeingly down at the pleats she had made on the sheets with nervous fingers. "I'm leaving, Tyler. I think that would be best."

"For whom?" he asked, tilting her chin up, forcing her to meet his steady gray eyes.

"For all of us."

"No. Not for Faith. Not for me."

"I think—"

"You think too much, Miss Ashton. That's your main problem." He kissed her again. This kiss lacked the ferocity of the former one, but was far sweeter. Lifting his head, he impaled her with his eyes. The intensity with which he had looked at her last night when she told him she loved him was there again.

"Our timing was off, Hailey, when you spoke of love. I never got to tell you how much I love you. At least not verbally. You *do* know, don't you, that I love you?"

Speech was beyond her, so she simply shook her head. "How could you not, Hailey?" he asked, genuinely perplexed. "Why do you think I pursued you so relentlessly? Why do you think I couldn't bear to have you out of my sight for more than a few hours at a time?"

"You led me to believe that your interest was in physical conquest and nothing else," she said, toying with the buttons of his shirt. One by one they began to slip free of the buttonholes.

"Maybe initially, but not after that business trip when I learned that having met you, I couldn't live without you. I knew then that you were no passing fancy in my life. Actually, I knew it the first time I saw you when you gave me such a hard time." He smiled tenderly and took her chin between his thumb and index finger. "I love you, Hailey. Say you'll marry me."

"Tyler," she breathed, reaching up to encircle his neck with her arms. She kissed him fervently, daringly, aggressively. "I love you, I love you, I love you. For so long I've wanted to tell you that."

"Since when?" he asked against the soft, satiny flesh of her neck.

"I think since I first saw you."

"How could you fall in love with a rude boor like that?"

She laughed, ruffling his hair with her fingers. "I

don't know, but the ruder and more boorish you became, the more I loved you."

"You're going to help me in my business, aren't you? You've done so well at Serendipity, I can't wait to turn you loose on the few kinks within the corporation."

"Won't your other employees resent interference from the boss's wife?"

"We can always live in sin," he said, winking lewdly. "Then you'd only be the boss's mistress."

"Not on your life. From now on, I'm going to be like a ball and chain around your neck. Besides, Faith— Oh, Tyler, where is she?"

He laughed at her guilty expression. "Despite the tumult last night, we both woke up early. She suggested that I talk to you before she offered her own apologies for the things she said last night. I called the Harpers, gave them a purely fictitious story, and imposed upon their hospitality. They were happy to have Faith as a guest until we pick her up later this afternoon. Tomorrow, we'll get married. I hope Faith can keep the secret that long. She's bursting to tell someone."

Hailey lay back huffily and crossed her arms over her chest. "Well, you certainly were confident of my answer if you told Faith we were getting married before you even asked me."

"Faith assured me you'd accept. She said she had a woman's intuition that you would."

"Is she really happy about it?"

"Almost as happy as I am."

She smiled as she ran her fingers along his lips. "And today, what do we do until it's time to pick up Faith?"

"Didn't I tell you? You have to go to work," he said, getting off the bed. His eyes ran the length of her body as he began removing his clothing slowly. "Your job assignment for today is to make the boss happy."

"What chores could I possibly do to make him happy?" she asked, batting her eyelashes.

"We'll take them in alphabetical order."

Lean and naked and hard with desire, he lay down beside her and took her in his arms. His kiss was deep, his tongue making promises of things yet to come.

"Do you get rid of this, or do I?" he asked, referring to her T-shirt.

"You do."

His smug grin warned her that she had made an ill-advised choice. His hands found the hem of the long shirt and eased it over her waist, up her rib cage, to the bottom of her breasts. He lowered his head and used his nose to nudge the soft cotton over her ripe flesh.

The slowness with which his lips skimmed over her skin maddened her. Her hands plowed through his thick dark hair. Her thighs tightened against his broad torso as he lay between them. Slowly he caressed her smooth skin, still warm from sleep. Only occasionally letting his tongue dart out for one quick taste, he nib-bled at the underside of her breasts.

Then his kisses grew more ardent, his mouth more demanding, his tongue less fleeting. His hands came up to examine what had been made damp by his kisses. He lifted her breasts, raising her nipples to aching peaks of longing with the finessing of his thumbs. He circled slowly, rubbed gently, tantalized, tormented, soothed.

Desire bloomed deep inside her, radiating outward until it weakened her limbs, tightened her chest and became an audible whimper in her throat. Answering her entreaty, he enclosed her nipple with his mouth. His tongue and teeth brought her to a greater height of arousal.

"Please, Tyler. Please."

"Not yet, my love." He peeled the T-shirt over her head. "I don't want to rush today. We've got the rest of our lives to love each other. Let me indulge myself."

"You're beautiful," she murmured, combing her fingers through the hair on his chest. She lifted her head to kiss his feverish flesh, to honor with her lips and tongue his hard, flat nipples. Her hands inched over the muscles of his hips and down the backs of his thighs.

"Perhaps I taught you too well," he groaned. "You make me weak with loving you, Hailey." His eyes devoured her nakedness. "Beautiful." Kneeling, he leaned forward to kiss the valley between her ribs. His breath was a caress in itself as his lips moved downward. He treated her navel to gentle love bites.

When he met the fragile barrier of her panties, he caught the lacy garment between his teeth and dragged it down over her obliging hips and thighs. Her breath escaped in a rapturous sigh when his lips paid homage to what the veil had screened. Neglecting nothing, he loved all of her.

The pleasure was too intense for her to sustain. She was perilously poised on the brink of either death or rebirth. Just before she fell into the abyss, she called his name.

Rising above her, with one swift thrust he filled the aching void in her body that he had created. "I love you, Hailey. I love you."

The stars fell around them and yet they survived, more alive than they had ever been. They were attuned to each sight, sound, taste, and touch of one another. Even when it was over, he didn't leave her, but stayed nestled in her entrapping warmth to savor her.

He kissed her behind her ear. "Do you mind living in Atlanta?"

"Not if that's where you're going to live." His eyebrows were studied by fondling fingers.

"We'll find a house we all like, where we'll make a new life together. The three of us." His lips skipped playfully across hers. "Or four. Or more."

She pushed against his shoulders. "Tyler? What are you saying?"

He laughed. "That Faith is already planning a slew of brothers and sisters."

"But I don't know if I can have a baby."

"Of course you can," he murmured softly, tenderly. "You do everything well, Red." Love was shining in his eyes as he whispered against her lips, "Some things you do exceptionally well."

More
Sandra Brown!

Please turn this page
for a
bonus excerpt
from

A KISS REMEMBERED

a new
Warner Book
available wherever
books are sold.

She had purposely chosen a seat near the back of the classroom in order to study him without being obvious. It was remarkable how unchanged he was. Physically, the ten years since they'd seen one another had enhanced his masculine appeal. During his twenties he had held the promise of being a magnetic, virile man; in his thirties that promise had been realized.

Shelley's pen scratched across her tablet as she took notes on his lecture. This was only the second week of the fall semester, but he was already well into the topics he wanted to cover before the final exams just before Christmas. He held the class's rapt attention.

The political-science courses were conducted in one of the oldest buildings on campus. Its ivy-covered walls suggested a prestigious East Coast university rather than a college located in a northeastern Oklahoma township. The age of the building, its pleasantly creaking hardwood floors, and high-ceilinged, hushed hallways lent it a sedate atmosphere that appealed to the prelaw students.

The instructor, Grant Chapman, was propped against the desk at the front of the classroom. The desk was solid oak. It had survived over thirty years of professors leaning against it and bore its years well.

As did the man, Shelley thought. Mr. Chapman was as muscularly solid as he had been ten years before. Many a young heart had fluttered when he played on the faculty basketball team against the varsity. Wearing basketball trunks and a tank top, Grant Chapman had rendered the girls of Poshman Valley High School breathless. Shelley Browning included. Ten years had only honed those sleek muscles to a mature strength.

Silver now threaded the dark hair that was just as carelessly styled as it had been then. There had been a stringent rule against long hair at Poshman Valley High School, and the handsome young civics teacher had been one of its most frequent violators.

Shelley could vividly remember the day she'd first heard of Grant Chapman.

"Shelley, Shelley, wait until you see the dreamy new government teacher!" It was enrollment day after summer vacation. Her friend's face was flushed with excitement as she ran up to greet Shelley with the news. "We have him second period and he's absolutely beautiful. And he knows that when you talk about Chicago you're not talking about a city in Illinois. He's young! Government's going to be a gas," the girl had squealed, running off to inform someone else of their good fortune. "Oh, and his name is Mr. Chapman," she had called over her shoulder.

Shelley now listened to the deep resonance of his voice as he answered a question from a student. But his thorough answer didn't register any more than had the question asked him. Shelley was concentrating only on his voice. Leaning over her desk and unobtrusively closing her eyes, she remembered the first time she had heard those low, well-modulated tones.

"Browning, Shelley? Are you here?"

Her heart had plummeted to her feet. No one wanted to be called on the very first day back to school. Twenty pairs of curious eyes were riveted on her. She raised a trembling hand. "Yes, sir."

"Miss Browning, you've already lost your gym shorts. You may pick them up in the girls' locker-room office. Miss Virgil sent a note."

The class broke up and there were several catcalls and whistles. She stammered a thank-you to the new teacher, her cheeks flaming scarlet. He'd think she was a ninny. Funny, his opinion had meant more to her then than had that of her peers.

As she filed out of class that day he had stopped her at the door. "I'm sorry if I embarrassed you," he said apologetically. Her girlfriends were standing by, wide-eyed and envious.

"That's all right," Shelley had said timidly.

"No, it's not. You get five grace points on the first exam."

She had never gotten those five extra points because she made a one hundred on the first exam and on most of them after that. Government was her favorite subject that semester.

"Are you talking about before Vietnam or after?" Mr. Chapman was currently asking the student who had inquired about the influence of public opinion on presidential decisions.

Shelley shifted back to the present. He'd never remember "Browning, Shelley" and her lost gym shorts. She doubted if he'd remember at all those four brief months he'd taught at Poshman Valley High School. Surely not after all he'd been through. One didn't climb up through the ranks of Congress to become a valuable senatorial aide by being sentimental. One didn't survive the public scandal Grant Chapman had survived by dwelling on incidents that had happened years earlier in a small farming community that played such an insignificant role in his colorful life.

Maybe that was why he seemed so unchanged to her. She had seen him on television often when reporters were still hounding him for a comment on the scandal that had rocked Washington society. She had studied the pictures of him accompanying the newspapers' headline accounts. Unflattering as newspaper pictures usually were, she could see no deterioration in the face that had emblazoned itself on her mind and refused, even after ten years, to be dismissed.

Shelley was sure he wouldn't know her. At sixteen she had been coltishly slender. No less svelte now, she was softer, rounder, fuller in a very feminine way. The years had melted away the childish plumpness in her face to leave behind an interesting bone structure. High cheekbones accentuated her smoke-blue eyes.

Gone were the long bangs that had characterized her schoolgirl hairstyle. Now her hair was swept back to show her finely arched brows and heartshaped hairline. A true brunette, she was blessed with richly textured hair that fell over her shoulders like dark wine with sunlight shimmering through it.

Gone was the round-cheeked girl in cheerleader's uniform. Gone also was the innocence, the idealism. The woman was all too aware of the world and its selfishness and injustice. Grant Chapman knew something of that, too. They weren't the same people they had been ten years before, and she asked herself for the thousandth time why she had signed up for his class.

"Consider President Johnson's position at that time," he was saying.

Shelley glanced down at her watch. Only fifteen minutes of the class remained and she had taken exactly two lines of notes. If she weren't careful, she wouldn't excel in this class as she had in the government class that first semester of her junior year.

She recalled a cold windy day after that season's first norther.

"Would you consider helping me grade papers a few afternoons a week?" he had asked.

She was wearing her current boyfriend's letter jacket and her hands were tightly balled into fists inside the deep pockets. Mr. Chapman had stopped her in the courtyard between the gym and the classroom building. His collar-length hair, a shade too long to meet the code, was whipping wildly around his head. Wearing only his sportcoat, he was hunched against the north wind.

"Of course if you'd rather not, just tell—"

"No, no," she rushed to say and licked her lips, hoping they weren't chapped and dry-looking. "Yes, I'd like to. If you think I can."

"You're my champion student. That was a super report you did on the judicial system."

"Thank you." She was flustered and wondered why her heart was pounding so. He was just a teacher. Well, not *just* a teacher.

"If you can grade the objective parts of the tests, I'll read the essays. It'll save me hours of time in the evenings."

She had wondered then what he did in the evenings. Did he see a woman? That had been the topic of speculation at many a slumber party. She'd never seen him in town with anyone.

One night when her family had gone to the Wagonwheel steak house to eat dinner he was there. Alone. When he'd spoken to her, she'd nearly died. She stumbled through introductions to her parents and he'd stood up to shake hands with her father. After they were seated her little brother had spilled his milk and she could have gladly strangled him. When she hazarded a glance toward Mr. Chapman's table, he had left.

"Okay. What days?"

He squinted his eyes against the sunlight, which was bright in spite of the cold. She could never quite decide if his eyes were gray or green or somewhere in between, but she liked the way his dark lashes curled up when his eyes were narrowed that way. "You tell me." He laughed.

"Well, I have cheerleading practice on Thursday because of the pep rallies on Fridays." Stupid! He knows when the pep rallies are. "I take piano on Tuesday." What does he care, Shelley? "I guess Monday and Wednesday would be best."

"That'll be fine," he said. "Whew, it's cold. Let's get inside."

She had nearly tripped over her own stumbling feet when he unexpectedly took her elbow and escorted her to the door of the building. By the time the metal door clanged shut behind them, she thought she might very well faint because he'd touched her. She never told any of her girl friends about that. At the time, it was too precious a secret to tell.

The afternoons spent quietly in his classroom became the pivot around which the rest of her life revolved. She agonized on the days she didn't go, and she agonized on the days she did until the last bell of the day rang. She tried not to rush through the emptying halls to his classroom, but was often breathless when she arrived. Sometimes he wasn't there, but had left her a stack of papers with instructions. She went about grading her classmates' work with a diligence she'd never applied to anything else in her life. Often when he joined her, he'd bring her a soda.

One day as she sat checking the papers with the red pencil he'd given her, he stood up from his desk, where he was reading through an indecipherable composition. He peeled the V-necked sweater he wore over his head. "I think they've got the heat too high in here. This school isn't doing its part to conserve energy."

At the time, she couldn't even admire his patriotic conscientiousness, for she was dazzled by him. He linked his fingers, turned his hands outward and stretched his arms high over his head, arching his back. She was spellbound by the play of muscles under his soft cotton shirt. He released his breath in a healthy sigh as he lowered his arms and rolled his shoulders in an effort to relax them.

Shelley dropped the red pencil, her fingers suddenly useless. Had her skin not been holding her together, she thought she would have melted over the desk. She became aware of a stifling heat that had nothing to do with the thermostat on the wall.

She left his classroom that day bewildered. Much as she wanted to be near him, she suddenly felt compelled to escape. But there was no escaping this assault on her emotions because the tumult was within herself. It was totally new and different and nothing in her dating experiences had prepared her for it. She couldn't identify it then. Only later, when she was older, was she able to define what she had felt that afternoon: desire.

During those days of late fall, he never treated her with anything but open friendliness. When her boyfriend picked her up after football practice to drive her home in his reconditioned Cougar, Mr. Chapman called, "Have fun," to them as they left.

"Before next session you might want to read the first

three chapters of the textbook. It's boring as hell, but it will give you good background information."

Shelley was yanked out of her revery by his words. He had one hip hitched over the edge of the desk, a posture that blatantly declared his sex. Shelley doubted that any woman in the room was immune to his overwhelming sexuality. A woman would have to be blind or senile not to be affected, and glancing around, Shelley saw none that fit that description.

Rather, she saw that the female members of the class were all in their late teens or early twenties. High firm breasts jutted braless under T-shirts, and well-shaped, athletic thighs were encased in tight designer jeans. There were skeins of long carelessly styled hair in varying shades of brown, auburn and gold. She felt old and dowdy by comparison.

As you are, Shelley, she reminded herself. She was wearing a sweater, cranberry in color, and she wore a bra beneath it. The sweater matched her textured hose and complemented the mid-calf-length gray wool skirt. At least she knew how to dress fashionably and wasn't consigned to the polyester set—yet.

At twenty-six she was second oldest in the class. A serious gray-haired gentleman was seated in the front row. He had taken copious notes while the young man in the cowboy hat sitting next to Shelley had peacefully napped during the entire hour.

"Good-bye," Mr. Chapman said when the bell rang. "Oh yes, would Mrs. Robins please stop by the desk?"

History was repeating itself.

Shelley all but dropped the armload of books she was gathering up when he made his request. Less interested than the classmates at Poshman Valley had been, the forty or so other students filed out of the classroom, most of them intent on lighting up their first cigarette in over an hour.

Head down, she concentrated on weaving her way through the maze of desks, less ordered than the neat rows in his classroom ten years ago. Out of the corner of her eye, she saw the last student leave the room. Negligently he let the door close solidly behind him. She stifled the insane impulse to ask him to please leave it open.

When she was a few feet away from his desk, when she had run out of excuses not to look at him, she lifted the screen of dark lashes from her eyes and met Grant Chapman's gaze fully for the first time in ten years.

"Hello, Shelley."

She gasped. Or at least she felt the soft gasp rise to her throat and only hoped later that she had caught it in time. "Hello, Mr. Chapman."

A chuckle formed in his throat, but he, too, stopped it before it made a sound. His wide, sensually molded lips smiled easily, but his eyes were busy taking an inventory of her face. They took note of her hair, the unknowingly vulnerable eyes, the slender elegance of her nose, her lips. He studied her lips for a long time, and when her tongue came out nervously to moisten them, she cursed it for doing so.

It was dangerously still and quiet in the room. He had come away from the desk to stand directly in front of her. He had always seemed so overwhelmingly tall. Not frighteningly so, but protectively so.

"I . . . I didn't think you'd know me."

"I knew you the first day you came to class." Standing close like this, his voice sounded huskier. When he projected it during one of his lectures, it lost the intimate pitch that was now wreaking havoc on her equilibrium. "I was starting to wonder if you were going to go through the entire semester without even saying hello."

Ten years of maturity were swept away by his gentle teasing and she felt as young and callow as the first day she met him.

"I didn't want to embarrass you by speaking and having you struggle to remember me. That would have put you in an awkward position."

"I appreciate your concern, but it was unnecessary. I remember you well." He continued to peruse her face analytically and she wondered if he thought the years had embellished or detracted from her features. She herself didn't feel that she had become less attractive or more so; she only knew she was different from the girl who had so painstakingly graded his papers.

Had he known about her infatuation for him? Had he discussed it with a lady friend? "You should see her, sitting there so prim and proper, her hands perspiring. Every time I move, she jumps like a scared rabbit." She imagined him shaking his head ruefully and laughing.

"Shelley?"

He routed her out of her unpleasant musing by speaking her name as though he'd had to repeat it several times. "Yes?" she asked breathlessly. Why was oxygen suddenly so scarce?

"I asked how long you've been Mrs. Robins."

"Oh, uh, seven years. But then I *haven't* been Mrs. Robins for two years."

His brows, which were a trifle shaggy and thoroughly masculine, lifted in silent query.

"It's a long, boring story." She glanced down at the toe of her flat-heeled cordovan shoe. "Dr. Robins and I parted company two years ago. That's when I decided to go back to school."

"But this is an undergraduate course."

Had any other man worn jeans and western boots with a sportcoat he would have looked as though he were imitating a film star, but Grant Chapman looked absolutely devastating. Did it have anything to do with the open throat of his plaid cotton shirt, which revealed a dark wedge of chest hair?

She forced her eyes away from it to answer him. "That's what I am. An undergraduate, I mean." She had no idea how delectable her mouth looked when she smiled naturally. For the last few years smiles hadn't come easily. But when they did, the weariness that had been etched on her face by unhappiness was relieved, and her lips tilted at the corners and were punctuated with shallow dimples.

Grant Chapman seemed intrigued by those indentations at either side of her mouth. It took him a long time to reply. "I would have thought that since you were such a good student, you would have gone to college as soon as you graduated from Poshman Valley."

"I did. I went to the University of Oklahoma, but ..." She glanced away as she remembered her first semester in Norman and how meeting Daryl Robins had changed the course of her life. "Things happen," she finished lamely.

"How are things in Poshman Valley? I haven't been back since I left. God, that's been ..."

"Ten years," she supplied immediately and then wanted to bite her tongue. She sounded like a good little girl giving her teacher the correct answer. "Something like that," she added with deliberate casualness.

"Yes, because I went to Washington directly from there. I left before the year was up."

Self-defensively she averted her eyes. The next hour of afternoon classes must have begun. Only a few students drifted by on the sidewalks outside the multipaned windows.

She couldn't talk about his leaving. He wouldn't remember, and she had tried for ten years to forget. "Things in Poshman Valley never change. I get back fairly often to see my folks. They still live there. My brother is teaching math and coaching football at the junior high."

"No kidding!" He laughed.

"Yes. He's married and has two children." She adjusted her armload of heavy books into a more comfortable position against her breasts. When he saw the gesture, he leaned forward to take them from her and set them on the desk behind him. That left her without anything to do with her hands, so she folded them awkwardly across her waist, hoping he wouldn't guess how exposed she felt.

"Do you live here in Cedarwood?"

"Yes. Since I'm going to school full-time, I rented a small house."

"An older one?"

"How did you know?"

"There are a lot of them here. It's a very quaint little town. Reminds me of Georgetown. I lived there the last few years I was in Washington."

"Oh." She felt terribly gauche. He had hobnobbed with the elite, the beautiful, the powerful. How provincial she must seem to him.

She made a move to retrieve her books. "I don't want to keep you—"

"You're not. I'm finished for the day. As a matter of fact, I was going to get a cup of coffee somewhere. Would you join me?"

Her heart pounded furiously. "No, thank you, Mr. Chapman, I—"

His laughter stymied her objection. "Really, Shelley, I think you can call me by my first name. You're not in high school any longer."

"No, but you're still my teacher," she reminded him, slightly perturbed that he had laughed at her.

"And I'm delighted to be. You decorate my classroom. Now more than ever." She wished he had kept laughing.

That was easier to handle than his intent scrutiny of her features. "But, please, don't categorize me as a college professor. The word 'professor' conjures up a picture of an absentminded old man with a headful of wild white hair searching through the pockets of his baggy tweed coat for the eyeglasses perched on top of his head."

She laughed easily. "Maybe you should try teaching creative writing. That was a very graphic word picture you painted."

"Then you get my point. Make it Grant, please."

"I'll try," was all she would promise.

"Try it out."

She felt like a three-year-old about to recite "Mary Had a Little Lamb" for the first time. "Really, I—"

"Try it," he insisted.

"Very well." She sighed. "Grant." The name came more easily to her tongue than she had imagined. In all her fantasies over the past ten years, had she called him by his first name? "Grant, Grant," she repeated.

"See? See how much better that is? Now, how about coffee? You don't have another class, do you? Even if you do, you're late, so ..."

Still she hesitated. "I don't—"

"Unless you'd rather not be seen with me." His change of tone brought her eyes flying up to his. The words had been spoken quietly, but there was a trace of bitterness lying just below the surface.

She caught his meaning instantly. "You mean because of what happened in Washington?" When he answered by silently piercing her with those gray-green eyes, she shook her head vehemently. "No, no, of course not, Mr. . . . Grant. That has nothing to do with it."

She was touched that his relief was so apparent. "Good." He raked strong, lean fingers through his hair. "Let's go for coffee."

Had the look in his eyes and that boyishly vulnerable gesture not compelled her to go with him, the urgency behind his words would have. "All right," she heard herself say before a conscious decision was made.

He smiled, turned to pick up her stack of books and his own folder of notes, and propelled her toward the door. When they reached it, he leaned across her back to switch off the lights. She was aware of his arm resting fleetingly on her back and held her breath.

For an instant, his hand closed around the base of her neck before sliding to the middle of her back. Though the gesture was nothing more than common courtesy, she was acutely aware of his hand through the knit of her sweater as they walked across the campus.

Hal's, that microcosm of society that is on every college campus in the country, was noisy, smoky, crowded. Neil Diamond was lamenting his loneliness from the speakers strategically embedded in the ceiling. Waiters with red satin armbands on their long white sleeves were carrying pitchers of draft beer to cluttered tables. Students of every description, from preppies and sorority girls to bearded intellectuals to muscled jocks, were smelted together in convivial confusion.

Grant took her arm and steered her to a relatively private table in the dim far corner of the tavern. Having secured them their seats, he leaned across the table and said in a stage whisper, "I hope I don't have to show my I.D." At her puzzled frown he explained, "I don't think anyone over thirty would be welcomed in here." Then, at her laughing expression, he clapped his hand to his forehead, "By God, you're not even thirty, are you? Why do I suddenly feel more and more like our white-haired, doddering professor?"

When the waiter came whizzing by, Grant slowed him long enough to call, "Two coffees."

"Cream?" the fleeing waiter asked over his shoulder.

"Cream?" Grant asked her. She nodded.

"Cream," he shouted to the waiter. "You weren't even old enough to drink coffee the last time I saw you, were you?" he asked her.

Not really listening to his question, she shook her head. She was having a hard time keeping herself from staring at him. His hair was attractively windblown. The open "V" of his shirt continued to bemuse her. Daryl Robins had thought himself the epitome of masculinity, yet his chest had had only a sprinkling of pale hair in the center, while this was a veritable forest growing from darkly tanned skin. An urge to reach out and touch it with her fingertips was so powerful, she looked away.

One glance around the room confirmed what she had suspected. Coeds were eyeing Grant with the unconcealed sexual interest of the modern woman. She was the subject of their cool appraisal. Grant Chapman was a celebrity in a notorious, dangerous way, with the kind of reputation no woman could resist being curious about. Shelley had tried to ignore the ripple of attention that their arrival had created, but the bold stares being directed toward them now were most disconcerting.

"You get used to it," he said softly after a moment.

"Do you?"

"No, you don't really get *used* to it, you just learn to live with it and ignore it if you can." He twirled a glass ashtray on the highly glazed wooden tabletop. "That's only one consequence of having your face in the news every day for several months. Whether you're the good guy or the bad guy, the culprit or the victim, guilty or innocent, notoriety shadows you. Nothing you do is private anymore."

She didn't say anything until after the harried waiter had served them their coffee. Shelley stirred cream into her cup and said gently, "They'll get accustomed to seeing you around. News that you'd be joining the faculty this fall spread through the campus like wildfire last spring. Once you're here for a while, the excitement will die down."

"My classes filled up quickly. I don't find that flattering. I realize most of the students who registered for them did so out of curiosity. I saw the cowboy sitting next to you sleeping today."

She smiled, glad that he didn't have that intense, guarded expression on his face any longer. "I don't think he appreciated the finer points of your lecture."

Grant returned her smile briefly and then gazed at her earnestly, searching the depths of her eyes with an intensity that made her quail. "Why did you take my class, Shelley?"

She looked down into her coffee; then, thinking that silence would incriminate her, she said spiritedly, "Because I needed the credit."

He ignored her attempted levity. "Were you a curiosity seeker, too? Did you want to see if I'd grown horns and a long tail since you'd seen me?"

"No," she cried softly. "Of course not. Never."

"Did you want to see if I'd remember you?" He was leaning forward now, his forearms propped against the edge of the table. The distance between them was visibly decreased, but rather than shrinking from him, she felt an irresistible urge to move closer still.

"I . . . I guess I did. I didn't think you would remember. It's been so long and—"

"Did you want to see if I remembered the night we kissed?"

SANDRA BROWN is the author of more than sixty books, of which over forty were *New York Times* bestsellers, including the #1 *New York Times* bestseller *The Alibi*, *Envy*, *The Switch*, *Standoff*, *Unspeakable*, *Fat Tuesday*, *Exclusive*, *The Witness*, *Charade*, *Where There's Smoke*, and *French Silk*. Her novels have been published in thirty languages. She and her husband divide their time between homes in Texas and South Carolina.